CHAT

Debbie Archer

DEDICATION

TO MACK...ALWAYS

ACKNOWLEDGMENTS

I could never have written without Jesus. I ask Him to grant me words He can bless. I pray my work will glorify Him. Thank you, Lord for placing the following people in my life to encourage and support me.

Mack, my best friend. You never cease to love me through another story. I am in awe of your patience, and I love you so very much.

To Mom for telling me I could write, and to Daddy who taught me art comes in many forms.

To all my precious friends across the years and to Saundra, without whom I would be lost. Your friendship is irreplaceable.

To those wonderful souls at Scotchwood Hill. Martha Rodriguez, I'd love to get inside your head and just crawl around for a while! Your cover art is beautiful. I am grateful for your artist's eye, your patience, your texts, and your loving friendship.

Pat, I've never met an editor as brilliant as you. The skills you've shared with me are greatly appreciated. I will carry them with me for the rest of my writing life. I am humbled by your amazing gifts—not only for your editing, but for your friendship.

To my writers' group—Writers Ink of NE Arkansas and the White County Creative Writers of Searcy, Arkansas. You folks mean business! I stand humbled when I'm among you, and I'm so blessed for the camaraderie you so freely offer. You're all BEAUTIFUL.

To Shelley Doyle, my hairdresser, who never fails to listen to my ideas and characters and helps me figure out sticky plot dilemmas. Congrats on winning the Character Naming Contest. Now your name appears in THIS book! Can't wait to use your winning contest entry name. Win win. ☺

To Rhonda Potter for your prayers and pure love of God, and to all my praying soul sisters and brothers. Prayers have been answered.

To my guardian animals who hole up with me when I write and love on me when I don't (and sometimes love on me *while* I'm writing).

Joyce Rose, thanks to you, I am living a life filled with joy and fulfilment. Had you not cared all those years ago, this writer would never have made it to college. Thank you for being my friend.

To Deb Blalock, you are God's gift to everyone. I may not get to see you in person very often, but not a day goes by that I don't think about you.

Claudia, thank you for your steadfast friendship. I love you.

Finally, to all my Facebook friends and encouragers: Thank you for caring and sharing, posting and commenting. Thank you for your reviews and your support.

Blessing to you all.

ONE

When I walked into the classroom Monday morning, I tried not to look at Bretta's chair. Instead, I focused on the faces of my classmates. Their gazes darted all over the room—except not at that empty chair. I guess they were tired of staring at the ceiling, the pencil sharpener, and the bulletin board with the calendar's dumb leprechaun on it, so when I got there, they all stopped and looked at me. But only for a second. Then they looked away.

They knew my best friend wasn't riding my heels, and they knew she wasn't going to be in that chair. Not first period. Not tomorrow. Not ever.

She was dead.

Making my way to my seat, I unzipped my backpack. The newspaper caught in the fastener. I nudged it deeper into the bag. When I thought of the article about Bretta, I felt a little sick to my stomach. Maybe coming today hadn't been such a great idea. I wished I could be invisible. I rubbed my hands on my jeans. They had a mustard stain on the knee, but I didn't care. I wore them the last time I saw Bretta.

I knew coming today wouldn't be easy, but I wasn't expecting it to be this bad. One time, when I was in kindergarten, I got tangled up in the stage curtains. I felt like I was going to suffocate. I remember talking to God and telling him I couldn't breathe. I did pretty much the same thing now only without opening my mouth. Squeezing my eyes shut, I took a deep breath and told Him I was scared. When I opened my eyes, the room was the same – bizarre quiet. A pin dropping would have sounded like somebody bludgeoning a drum. But at least I could breathe.

I fumbled around in my bag, pretending to look for a pencil. It was the easiest way to keep my mind diverted. Diverted. Rhymes with perverted. *Pervert.* I'd heard the word a million times in fourteen years. Kids say it all the time at school. You bump into somebody, they call you a pervert. Somebody's in a bad mood—they call you a pervert. At some point, the word starts to sound almost as normal as hello. I wonder if these people knew what it really meant. I didn't until yesterday. I'll think more about what I call someone from now on. I'll think more about a lot of things from now on.

That word appeared in the newspaper article about Bretta's attacker. Perverted. I wish I'd never heard of it.

Mrs. Bentley, our English teacher, walked in. She stopped in the doorway and looked at the empty chair in front of me, adjusting the folder she carried. She walked across the room, heels smacking the concrete floor. She placed the folder on her desk and stared at it, as if daring it to move without her permission.

"Robert," she said curtly, "take the chair in front of Rachel McNeely and put it in the back of the room."

Robert jumped like somebody slapped him. He looked at the chair, then at Bentley. Robert wasn't one to disobey. He was the true, prude, teacher's pet, but Bentley's order bothered him. He looked at me and then back at her.

"Well," she demanded, placing her hands on her hips. "What's wrong? I want that chair moved now. Do you understand?"

Robert nodded and pulled his body out of his seat. I was biting my lip. I thought I'd cried all I could, but here I was on the verge of leaking again. I kept my head down while Robert lifted the chair and carried it across the room. I pretended to be wiping hair out of my eyes, but it wasn't hair. It was a good thing I didn't have on mascara. I followed Robert's movements with blurry eyes. For once my stringy bangs came in handy. He put Bretta's desk beside the closet door. I looked in front of me. There was a gaping hole in the line of desks. I gave my lip one last nip and looked at the hole. There was one exactly like it in my heart.

"Rachel, move up," Mrs. Bentley barked.

"What?" I couldn't have heard her right. My heart lurched.

"I said," she said sternly, "advance your seat." Then she turned around and started to write on the board. I sat too long, I guess, because when she turned around, she was mad. I can always tell when Bentley is mad. She gets this pucker between her eyebrows, and it's deep. She gets that pucker a lot—maybe that's why it's turned into a permanent crease. Seeing her lose her temper isn't anything new. We've all seen it before. It's usually because of something stupid one of the guys in the room has said. They can be lame. Sometimes she gets mad over an announcement from the intercom or some other interruption. Those are things I can't control, but I don't want her to be annoyed with me. I don't like it when people are mad at me. I guess it's a flaw or something, but I can't stand it.

When I look up, she's staring at me.

"Rachel, please move your seat. If it's too heavy, Robert can move it for you," she said quietly. But it wasn't a thoughtful kind of quiet. It was the kind of quiet you hear just before a tornado comes through and blows out all your windows.

"The seat isn't too heavy, Mrs. Bentley," I muttered. "I just don't want to sit there."

"I see," she nodded. The nod was slow. Her gray eyes bore into my brown ones. I could feel my face turning red and every freckle on my face was burning like neon dots. Even the cross earrings I wore seemed to tingle hot on my earlobes. She was ticked now, and I was the one who had done it. Turning her back to us, she began writing more words on the board. The sound from the chalk slashing at the board was obvious. "Pam, please trade seats with Rachel and move your new seat up in the line. Then I want everyone in that row to move up one space." The words were sharp and clipped.

The sound of the chalk continued to echo through the room. Every other teacher in the school had switched from the old chalkboards. Not Mrs. Bentley. I guess she liked the sound of the chalk scratching across the board. She'd been known to run her fingernails down the green finish if the class seemed to be drifting off. You can't do that with a white board.

Pam Nichols sat across from me. I looked at her and then back to Bentley. Pam shrugged an apology, and I could tell she didn't want to move. She mouthed, "I'm sorry," and got up from her seat. She's a tall girl like me. But no one ever teases her about her height because she's the best eighth grader on the girls' basketball team. Everyone likes Pam because she's pretty and friendly. At that minute, I liked her because she understood how hard this was for me. She didn't want to move. She just didn't have a choice.

In less than a minute, we swapped seats. In even less time, Pam moved into Bretta's spot in line. Everyone behind her scooted into place. When the shuffling ended, Mrs. Bentley stopped writing and turned around. Her face wasn't exactly transformed, but the trench was gone. A knock at the door took care of that.

Heaving a huge sigh, she clacked over to the door. I couldn't help but stare at the shoes she was wearing. She still dressed like one of those women from the sixties shows. No one would ever catch her in a pair of jeans and stylish sneakers. The closest thing to jewelry she owned was a pair of glasses that swung from a tacky black rope around her neck. Her shoes were just as black and just as tacky. Fashion wasn't her strong point. As far as I knew, the only really cool thing she owned was her car. Everybody said she got a new one every few years. This year's was an emerald green BMW. Guess she could afford it. She sure didn't spend money on anything nice to wear.

She and her clacking shoes arrived at the door. As she opened it, we could see Mr. Jennings, our principal, standing in the hall. The last time he'd come by the rooms was about a break-in at school. This time, he spoke in quiet tones and looked at Mrs. Bentley like he was worried about her. I looked at the people around me. Everybody was straining to hear the conversation at the door. I was pretty sure it was about Bretta. Was there news about the person responsible? Maybe Mr. Jennings was coming around to tell the teachers what to do. Maybe he was coaching her about what to say. Mr. Jennings is at least 6'5" and is one muscled-up principal. The guys on our wrestling team don't look as buff as he does. He's nice too, but he can be intimidating. Even the worst kids don't like to get sent to his office.

Bentley gave her head one vigorous nod and then practically shut the door in Mr. Jenning's face. She's the only teacher in school who would have the guts to brush off her boss that way. But Bentley has guts. Even an idiot wouldn't mistake her for a sweet little old lady with gray hair. Anybody who takes the time to look into her eyes knows that kind is not a word that describes Bentley. Whatever kindness she ever had was long gone, tucked away in a secret, safe place. Padlocked.

She probably saw Bretta's murder as an imposition.

I wanted to hit her for being so selfish. Closing my eyes, I took another deep breath. Fingering one of the small cross earrings, I prayed for two things – that the day would go by fast and that I would get a grip.

Once she got back to her podium, she looked odd, like she was trying to decide what to say. Her cheeks flushed an ugly magenta color, and she blinked faster than usual. It was like the words she'd started to say flew right out the door with Mr. Jennings, and she couldn't decide what to say in their place. I guess she finally figured it out. When her message fell out of her mouth, it wasn't what any of us expected.

"I want all the information on the board to be covered tonight, and you may use the remainder of this class period. I have Power Point handouts you may use as a study guide for the upcoming test. Lucy, come forward and pass these out. If any of you lose your copy, you will be responsible for obtaining another. Sign the sheet Lucy has in her hand. This states you have received this study guide. If you can't keep up with this one, the same guide appears on my web page. But I don't want anyone using the excuse that their computer is down, or they couldn't get to a computer and therefore couldn't print this out. So, I'm providing you with one today. I will double check to make sure everyone has signed they've received a copy." Then she turned around, sat at her desk, and pulled out writing prompts that had been turned in last week. She began marking the papers in front of her.

That was it. She wasn't going to tell us what Mr. Jennings said. The rest of the class relaxed. I didn't. I was sure he had said something about Bretta. Everybody else was relieved. Normally, I would have been, too, because the worst part of her class is when she calls us up individually to go over our mistakes. But nobody seemed to mind today. Compared to what happened over the weekend, getting chewed out for the misuse of a dangling participle didn't seem so bad.

Twenty more minutes dragged by. She didn't say anything about Bretta. But I did notice when she picked up a piece of notebook paper, her hand shook. Bending toward the paper shredder beside her desk, she hesitated, and then drew back. She tucked the paper on the bottom of her stack—not before I saw the back of the paper. It had a two-inch calligraphy B in the top left-hand corner. Bretta's personal signature. Mrs. Bentley glanced in my direction and flinched when she found I was watching her. Again, our eyes locked, but this time she was the first to look away.

Five minutes before class was over, she picked up the notebook she'd carried with her. Grabbing up a stack of pamphlets, she asked Kevin to hand them out. When everyone had one in their hand, she stood and cleared her throat.

"There is to be an art competition held in this region. The work of several students will be used in a traveling exhibition in the South. Schools throughout the nation have received similar contest guidelines

6

throughout the year. Our administration believes this is a worthwhile venture that will benefit the students of Seely. Many schools in Arkansas have chosen not to participate due to the upcoming benchmark exams. We believe our students will flourish with added responsibilities."

Like we needed more responsibilities. Major laugh! I thought we had all the responsibility we could deal with—especially now. But, looking at the faces around me, maybe I wasn't seeing it the same way as everybody else.

"The winner will have his or her work displayed and will be awarded five thousand dollars," she announced. She stopped and rolled her eyes as the room erupted with surprised comments. After a few minutes, she picked up a wooden paperweight—everyone called it the Bentley Gavel and banged it against the desk. The room went silent. Every eye was on her. Five thousand dollars was a lot of money, and it had everyone's attention. Even those who couldn't draw a stick figure wanted that money.

"In light of the deadline, you may wish to begin working on an idea soon. The project or piece cannot be computer generated, and it must be of your own creation. The information has been on the internet for quite some time, and our school received the posters and pamphlets several weeks ago, but *most* of the faculty wished to discuss the pros and cons before handing out information to the students. According to the contest rules, staff members are only allowed to offer rules and regulations. The premise of the piece must remain solely your work. If entering the contest, you will be expected to turn in your work to any teacher within two weeks. That will be just prior to our Easter break, which will allow adequate time to catalog and number each entry." She paused to glare at the entire room full of excited faces. "This is to be done on your own time, without your parents' help. Also, you are not to forget your responsibilities in tending to your regular assignments."

How could any of us forget? That's all we'd heard since we'd set foot in her class. Information is vital. Learning is living. Education will prepare you for life. Yawn, blah, yawn. She must think she's the poster chick for school slogans. Parents loved her. Students didn't.

"I realize the money is a grand incentive," she continued, "but you must have your priorities in order. Your standard of learning is something you've been striving toward since kindergarten. Most of you," she stopped to glare at those unfortunate enough to be repeating her class, "have learned study skills, test-taking skills, and more importantly, self-discipline. You should be proud of this. Do not allow yourself to become sidetracked by the lure of the contest money."

Looking like someone had pulled her plug, she turned around and walked toward the door. It was like telling us about this contest had been the hardest job she ever had. I wondered why she was so rigid— what a perfect word for her. Rigid. I liked the way it stood up straight in my mind. In all the months I'd been in her class, I couldn't remember seeing her smile once. Something or someone had stolen every ounce of her humor, and she was determined to steal ours.

Out of nowhere, my anger reared up again. I wanted her to say *something* about Bretta. Some part of me needed to know other people missed her. So far, no one had even mentioned her name. It was like everyone was trying to pretend she never existed. I knew it was because they didn't know what to say, but I needed to hear words.

I looked around. Some were already sketching ideas; others were sticking their information sheets away to look at later. Clutching the brightly colored brochure in my hand, I gazed at the spot where Bretta's desk used to be. She would have loved this. She dreamed of being an artist when she grew up. But she wouldn't grow up.

She was dead.

TWO

*F*orty minutes before school ended for the day, Mr. Keely, my math teacher, sent a message to the computer I was on. I'd just finished my math quiz and punched the print button. I heard the printer on his desk spitting out my paper just before I saw the message on my monitor. He waited until I finished with my test to send the note.

Mr. Keely taught advanced math classes. Guess my I.Q. kicked in the day I tested. So had Bretta's, which was funny because she hated math. We were both in Pre-AP math and extra fine arts classes because we were in the school's gifted and talented program. But there was one big difference. The only class Bretta really liked was art. I liked the math class okay, but my passion was creative writing. Bretta loved canvases. I loved words.

By the time I got to Mr. Keely's class, I was tired. We all were. We must have looked because he didn't make us do a lot of work other than the quiz. As teachers go, he was cool. He could have called me to the front of the room and told me to go to the counselor's office, or he could have announced it in front of the class. Not Mr. Keely. He's good with awkward. When somebody's upset, he draws attention away from that person. If someone has to go to the bathroom, he nods toward the door. Some kids take advantage of that, but only the jerks.

When the bell rang, I headed out into the hall and turned left.

I'd been expecting this all day—and dreading it. It's not that I don't like our counselor, Mrs. Shelly Doyle. She's a nice lady. But even with Mrs. Doyle, I couldn't talk about Bretta.

I hadn't been able to talk to anybody. Not Mom. Not Aunt Jane. Not Dad. Especially not Dad. Besides, he was a whole coast away. His way of communicating was to send an e-mail, and even those had almost stopped. Even texting was too personal for Dad. I guess he was afraid I might call him if he sent me a text message. No chance. He didn't know about Bretta yet. Or maybe he did and just didn't care.

I jostled my way toward Mrs. Doyle's office, dodging a couple of kids carrying a catapult, and then I ran into a whole herd of freshmen trying to get to the auditorium for the big meeting. An announcement had been made during break. All students were to attend. I knew it was about Bretta's murder and was pretty sure Mrs. Doyle had chosen now to talk to me, so I wouldn't have to sit through the meeting with everyone staring at me.

Almost everybody knew I was Bretta's best friend. That's why they had been watching me all day. Some of them worried I would fall apart. Others were probably disappointed I hadn't. I was cheap entertainment, and because I wasn't sure how I was supposed to act, I felt guilty. But that wasn't the biggest reason my gut was twisted in knots.

The door to her office was open when I got there. I stepped inside and walked through her outer office checking out the new chairs and couch she'd added. It looked like a nice room to hang out in. I guess that was the mood she was going for. I mean, it is a counselor's office. She's kind of like a student shrink. Stepping inside her private office, I waited. I looked at posters on her wall, where I saw the flier about the art contest was tacked to a corkboard.

"I'm afraid I messed up," Mrs. Doyle said behind me. I jumped and turned to look at her. "Evidently, I wasn't supposed to post that until today. There was a big discussion about whether or not our kids would be allowed to enter because of the testing schedule coming up.

10

I gave one of the fliers to Bretta last month." She shrugged. I liked that she hadn't hesitated to say Bretta's name out loud. I relaxed a little.

"Yeah, I got one today from Mrs. Bentley," I said. I looked at the messy desk. For some reason, it made me feel better. I sat in the nearest chair.

"Rachel," she said. Her voice was quiet, but Mrs. Doyle's quiet was soothing. No windows would be busting out from her tone. I focused on the blue eyes looking at me across the desk.

"Yes, ma'am." I realized I was sitting on the edge of the metal chair so I scooted back, holding on to the arms of the chair. Mrs. Doyle's eyes looked like mine probably did. Mom is always saying I can't fool her. My eyes give me away. Mrs. Doyle's eyes were like that. Hurt showed in her hazel eyes. Is that what she was seeing in mine? Was she seeing the rest of it, too? I looked away.

"Rachel, I know this is difficult. Losing a best friend is never easy, but to lose one in such a violent way hurts so much more."

I felt hot tears stinging my eyes again. If the floor would open up and swallow me in one big gulp, that would be just dandy.

"Have you talked to anyone about it?" Mrs. Doyle asked. I shook my head.

"Do you want to talk to me about Bretta? You know anything you tell me will be between you and me. It won't go any further."

I didn't doubt that. I trusted her, but I couldn't tell anyone my feelings. I wasn't sure myself. My friend was dead, and she'd been alive two days ago. But now everything was different.

My hands hurt. When I looked down, I saw my knuckles had gone white from gripping the chair arms. I let go and put my hands in my lap.

"What happened isn't your fault. You do know that, don't you?" she asked.

I managed to look at her and then down at my hands. "I guess." I could hear her shifting in her chair and sneaked a look at her. But she wasn't looking at me. She was looking at my backpack. I looked down quickly to see if the newspaper was sticking out.

"How much do you know about what happened, Rachel?" she asked.

I shrugged my shoulders. "I know she's gone," I answered. "but it's like I still expect to see her. I know she's dead. I understand that. I just can't seem to get my brain to know that." I sounded like a moron.

"You're still in denial, Rachel. That's completely normal. It's just one of the stages of grieving we all go through. You're supposed to feel this way. And," she said, leaning forward, "don't be surprised if you get angry. That's normal too."

I nodded. That was good to know, but she had no idea how *not* normal this whole situation was. I wasn't going to be the one to tell her. Instead, I just nodded. "One of her thumb drives is still in my locker, and I don't know what to do with it. I meant to give it to her last Friday when she came over, but…" I shrugged. I knew I was babbling, but I didn't know what else to do. My insides were starting to feel like Jello, and I wanted to be gone. The smothery feeling was coming back. Was this what it was like to have a panic attack?

Mrs. Doyle tilted her head forward like she was thinking. Her hair fell across her shoulders. She had the kind of hair that looked blonde and brown at the same time. Bronzed.

When I looked up, I noticed she looked even tinier behind her desk than in the hallway. She stood there a lot between classes and visited with the kids and teachers. Mostly the kids. She was friendly and easy to talk to.

Our last counselor retired last year and Mrs. Doyle came to Seely Junior High fresh out of college. Along with her new job, she had a new husband, Leo, who picked her up every afternoon after school. I wondered if he was as friendly as she was. It was hard to imagine her with somebody who wasn't. Both had just started going to my church and it probably wouldn't be long before they were involved in our church activities. Guess I'd find out more about him then.

"Would you like for me to give it to her family? I'd be happy to do that. I'm going by their house on my way home today."

"Sure," I blurted. "I'll go get it for you." Here was my chance. Grabbing my backpack, I was halfway out the door and headed down the hall before she could blink. I stopped in front of my locker and tried hard to stop my heart from pounding. Harvey, the vending machine guy, offered me juice from his machine, but I shook my head and concentrated on opening my combination. He gave me a smile and slammed the door on the machine in the hall. I took a deep breath. I'd made it this far today. I was not going to lose it now.

I must have rummaged around in my locker for quite a while because all of a sudden the dismissal bell rang. Students poured out of the auditorium. Some stopped when they saw me. Pam Nichols came over and sort of patted me on the shoulder. She acted like she wanted to say something, but I could tell she didn't know what words to use. The same students who had bumped into me earlier were walking way around me now, looking embarrassed.

Finding the thumb drive, I held it for a second. Feeling it. Sighing, I turned around and walked back toward Mrs. Doyle's office. Mr. Jennings was leaning against her door. Both stopped talking as I hurried up.

"Thank you, Mrs. Doyle," I said, shoving the thumb drive in her direction. "I really appreciate it." Rushing toward the door, I didn't look back, but I knew both adults were watching me. I'd never been so glad to see an exit sign in my life. I pushed the door open.

For a minute, I didn't understand what was going on. I stood there with my mouth open. It looked like every car in the entire county was there. Since we lived in a little town, most of us walked to and from school. The rest rode the bus or got a ride with friends. Today, dozens of cars were trying to squeeze in wherever they could. Some were parked on the shoulder of the road. Others pulled in people's front yards and were waving their arms, trying to get the attention of the kid they were there to pick up. A police car inched down the street.

I hadn't expected Mom to pick me up, and from the looks on the faces around me, the other kids hadn't expected their parents either.

Then it dawned on me. Nobody wanted us walking home today. Something in our town had shifted. One of our own had died. Horribly. Everything changed on Saturday when Bretta was murdered.

I felt my phone vibrate in my pocket, and at the same time, I spotted Mom at the end of the pick-up lane. Digging it out, I turned it off silent. "Hello," I said.

"Rachel. I'm picking you up today. I'll be there in a minute."

"Mom," I started. But then I realized she'd already disconnected. She hated it when people talked on their cell phones while driving. I could see her car, and technically, she wasn't driving. She was crawling.

It took almost ten minutes for her to get to where I was. I'd gotten tired and plopped down on the ground. When she pulled up, I hauled myself into the front seat. Since I don't carry a purse, I usually stuff everything into my backpack. I was about to do that with my phone when I remembered the newspaper article. Instead, I shoved the phone in my pocket.

Then I waited for her to ask about my meeting with Mrs. Doyle. I was sure she set it up for the counselor to talk to me. She was probably waiting for me to tell her about it. I wasn't going to do that. I'd wait for her to try and weasel it out of me. She'd probably try something clever, thinking I wouldn't know what she was doing. But the question never came. I kept glancing at her, but she kept her eyes on the road, looking in my direction every few seconds like she expected me to blow up. Finally, she smiled.

"I guess I'm a little nervous," she admitted.

"That's okay," I muttered. I didn't know why, but I was mad that she was picking me up. I felt like some little kid. My hands stung. Looking down, I saw my knuckles were white again. I unclenched them and stretched out my fingers. She didn't bring up Mrs. Doyle. Neither did I. If she didn't know about it, I wasn't going to tell her. Leaning back, I rubbed at the mustard stain on my jeans.

She smiled then, but it didn't look natural. It was a tired, up all-night kind of smile, and I felt bad about being mad. It wasn't her fault.

Mom didn't cause what happened to Bretta. Maybe this was part of that anger thing Mrs. Doyle had talked about. Knowing about it, though, didn't stop me from feeling it, but at least I could try to control it. I decided to cut my mom some slack. I knew she had a hard time deciding what would be best for me today—send me to school and back into a routine or keep me home so I could fall apart whenever the urge hit. She wanted things to be normal again. That was a laugh.

I read a book once by Truman Capote about a nice, normal family who were good, trusting people. They felt so safe that they never locked their doors. They were all murdered one night by two men who decided they wanted to kill people. Capote nailed it. The problem with feeling safe was that it caused people to let their guard down. Once their guard was down, things could happen. Awful things. Like with those people in Capote's book. Like with Bretta.

When we got home, I went straight to my room. I didn't stop to say anything to Aunt Jane. I wanted to be alone.

I went to my computer. Anger bubbled up inside me. Staring down at the laptop, I wanted to kick it—slash out and knock it off the desk. Instead, I reached down and turned it on. Then off. I backed away, staring at its black screen. Computers were like people. They could do wonderful things. They could also host some dangerous demons. It all depended on the person punching the buttons.

At 6:00 p.m., Mom knocked on my door to tell me dinner would be at 6:30. Aunt Jane always picked the menu on Monday, which meant meatloaf, green peas, and scalloped potatoes. I said I wasn't hungry, but that didn't work. The rule in our house is everyone shows up at the dinner table. No matter what.

After the meal was over and the dishes were washed, I went back to my room to finish the rest of my homework. I never thought I'd be glad for homework, but the truth was, it kept me from thinking about other stuff—mainly Bretta. By eight, it was all finished. Mom came in to see if I was warm enough. Five minutes later, she came in to turn on my nightlight. I was surprised to see the bulb still worked. That's how long it had been since I'd switched it on. I was climbing into bed after a hot shower when she came in a third time. She smoothed back my hair and kissed me goodnight— again like I was some little kid.

I think that's what she really wanted to do the first two times. She needed to touch my face and know I was okay. I had a picture in my head of parents all over town doing the same thing. I guess I'd do that, too, if I had a kid whose classmate had just been murdered. Maybe I'd sleep on the floor beside them.

When I heard her talking to Aunt Jane downstairs, I was sure she wasn't coming back. Flipping on my bedside lamp, I reached under my bed and pulled out my backpack. I unzipped the bag and pulled out the newspaper. It was a copy of the Sunday paper. The same article I read yesterday, without Mom knowing. She'd have a fit if she knew I'd read the article about Bretta's murder. That's why I carried it to school with me this morning. When I first read the article, I was so sick I wanted to throw up. The things that had been done to Bretta were too horrible. If it was that hard for *me* to read, I wondered how her parents felt when they opened up the paper and read it?

At least they wouldn't feel responsible!

I pulled the article in front of my face and made myself read it again. It was necessary. The same sickening image I had the first time I'd read it returned

Fourteen-Year-Old Girl Slain

The mutilated body of 14 year-old Bretta Deevers was found in Sherman Park Saturday evening. She was discovered after her parents notified the police of her absence. Signs indicate the young girl struggled with her attacker. The body has been sent to the state medical examiner for an autopsy to determine the cause of death, The body will be released to her family upon completion of the examination.

Authorities urge anyone with any information to

contact the local police immediately. Sheriff Harold was quoted as saying that "such a perverted crime has never taken place in Seely. We must catch whoever committed this heinous offense. We intend to catch the monster who killed the young girl."

The story laid out the details of her injuries. It went on to detail her injuries. Bretta's throat had been badly bruised and multiple stab wounds were mentioned. The article didn't mention where the wounds were, but the reporter it did say evidence she fought with her assailant was clear. Of course, when a girl is only 5'3" and skinny, there's not much hope - especially if the attacker is taller and stronger. On top of that, she thought she was meeting a friend.

When had she figured out she was going to die? When did it click that she couldn't trust the person looking into her eyes? Had she prayed? I clutched the paper and closed my own eyes.

The thing that bothered me the most was the picture below the text. Bretta wasn't in the photo, of course. Not even the media was that cold. Or maybe they were, but the authorities hadn't allowed them to snap a picture of Bretta's body.

The thing that tore parts of my brain into shreds lay beside the crime scene tape. One item. Size six. A new plaid running shoe marked the place where my friend died. I guess the photographer snapped the picture before the investigators took the shoe and anything else they could use as evidence.

I rammed the newspaper back into my backpack and slid it under the bed. My fingers touched my journal. I pulled it out and placed it in my lap.

Leaning over, I reached for my pen. Then I did the same thing I always do when I put an entry in. I reached for the dictionary on the bottom shelf of my nightstand. The book was an old, unabridged edition Mom and Aunt Jane had picked up at a yard sale. The damaged book hadn't sold in the shop, so I brought it home and adopted it. It was big and bulky with an old worn cover, and I liked it.

I started journaling when I was ten. For about four years now, I used the dictionary to find a new word to weave into my entries. This habit was a holdover from my old fourth grade teacher, Mr. Finch. He got me started on journaling. He also hooked me up with dictionaries. I liked hunting up new words that other people don't use a lot. Maybe that's why I love words. There's something cool about finding that perfect word that describes what I'm feeling.

I lost count of how many times I've been through the dictionary now. I liked to go in alphabetical order. It seemed orderly. Sometimes I found interesting words, but they don't fit what I was writing about. When that happens, I just jotted the word at the bottom of my entry. Tonight I was looking for only one word. It had to be perfect.

I flipped the dictionary open to the D page, ran my finger down each column and searched. Page after page, I studied the words. Then, on the fifth D page, I found it. It summed up the feeling in my gut. The minute I saw the word, spelled out in bold, black letters, I felt relieved. I knew other people had felt this way, otherwise, there wouldn't be a word set aside for it. They'd given it a name. **Desolate. Devastated, feeling abandoned as by friends, to forsake.**

I opened my journal to the next blank page and began to write.
Monday p.m. 9:05

I let Bretta down. Maybe I'm still letting her down because I'm not strong enough to tell people what really happened. I think maybe I'm a coward because I'm afraid of the consequences. I feel so **desolate.**

Is this how Bretta felt when she realized she was going to die?
I didn't mean for things to end up like this.

"I'm sorry, Bretta," I whispered. "I'm so sorry."

THREE

*T*he scream that ripped through the house jarred me out of my sleep. I was on my feet heading for the door. Mom came in, clutching her robe.

"Are you okay?" she asked. I nodded and hurried down the stairs to Aunt Jane's room. Mom was behind me. We could hear the whimpering from the hallway before we got there. Mom turned the knob and opened the door a few inches. As usual, the dim light in Aunt Jane's bathroom was on. Its glow was just enough to show Aunt Jane lying in her four-poster bed.

"Should I call the doctor?" I asked.

"She's still dreaming," Mom nodded. I looked at Aunt Jane's left hand and saw that she was clenching and unclenching her fist around her bedclothes. Her right hand lay motionless.

"Look out," Aunt Jane groaned. "I don't understand. You're wrong. I'm going …"

"Mom," I whispered.

She put her finger up to her lips. I got the message and shut my mouth. After a few minutes, she whispered, "Why don't you go back to bed, Rachel? There's nothing you can do. This is the same dream, and there's no reason for both of us to be here. She's always a little disoriented for a bit afterward, and then she's okay. I want to be here when she wakes up. Go on, honey. You'll have to get up in a few hours."

"No. I want to be here," I said. "It's not fair. Isn't there someone who could help her get rid of these dreams?"

Mom looked at the floor without answering. Was she avoiding my question? When she didn't answer, we both turned to look at Aunt Jane. Her head moved from side to side, and her grip on the bedspread was more urgent. Mom and I had seen this hundreds of times over the years. We knew the dream was almost over, which meant the worst was coming. I glanced at the landline by her bed. Mom saw me and shook her head.

"No. She doesn't want us to call Doctor Elders. We'll give her something when she wakes up." I went to the bathroom, ran a glass of water, and reached into the medicine cabinet for her migraine medicine. Once the glass was full, I turned the hot faucet full blast. It would take forever. The old house we lived in was kind of pathetic. It only had one hot water heater, and it was at the other end of the house. Mom wanted to add another, but there never seemed to be a good time to do that. Aunt Jane never fussed about anything. She was the sweetest woman I knew—besides Mom.

Tapping my foot, I waited for the water to heat up. As I waited, I looked around the tiny bathroom and stared at the snapshot beside Aunt Jane's medicine cabinet. Bretta smiled at me from the picture. She was holding a vintage paint set Aunt Jane had given to her for a birthday present. I'd forgotten about the gift and the picture.

The water scalded my hand. I rang the washcloth out and hurried back to Mom. She would put the cloth over Aunt Jane's eyes when she woke up. It always seemed to ease the headache that trailed her nightmares.

The moaning began. In a creepy way, it was like a Halloween sound. It sent shivers down my spine. She was so miserable. For six years, she'd had the same nightmare. Her terror was hard to watch—and to listen to. A person should become used to it, but I hadn't.

Neither had Mom.

"NOOOO! Aunt Jane shrieked, her right hand limp beside her. Her left hand covered her usually gorgeous face. She was looking around.

"It's okay, Jane," Mom soothed. "It's Lizzie and Rachel. Shhh. You're fine now. It was just a bad dream."

I looked at Mom. Her patience should be tapped out by now. She almost never lost her cool, though. I was a little jealous of that.

"Lizzie?"

"It's me. Here, let me put this over your eyes. You relax and lie back, and this will help. Does your head hurt?"

Aunt Jane nodded. She looked at her right hand. Closing her eyes, she fell back on the bed and reached for the warm washcloth. I knew that underneath the cloth, tears were in her eyes. Her gown was drenched in sweat. I reached into her dresser drawer and pulled out a crisp, clean one for her to change into. She took the cloth off her eyes and looked at me.

"Oh, Rachel. I'm so sorry, honey. This was your first day back to school, and I've gotten you up in the middle of the night." She looked miserable. I knelt beside her.

"You worry too much. I had plenty of sleep. I went to bed early."

"You have always been a terrible liar." She smiled and shifted in the bed. "I don't understand why I'm still having these stupid nightmares." She took the cloth off and glanced at her right hand again.

"I think you're doing too much," Mom said briskly.

"Me, too," I agreed.

Aunt Jane smiled and accepted the gown I held out. "I'm only doing my part. I *will* pull my weight around here," she said stubbornly. "You two have been so good to me since the accident. I don't intend to sit around taking up space. That's never been my style, and I don't intend to change." She frowned from the pain in her head and closed her eyes for a moment. "Besides, Liz," she said more quietly, "it works out well, the way you and I have been doing things." She paused and looked at Mom. "You do think it's working, don't you?" she asked anxiously.

"You know it is," Mom said, patting her shoulder. "But I don't want you overdoing it and making yourself sick. You go to all those auctions, and estate sales involves a lot of traveling. Then you come back and clean everything up and get it ready to display and sell. Just doing all the research on the pieces you buy takes a lot of time. Good grief, what you do is the hardest part! For all we know, all that research may be what's triggering your headaches. You're bent over books and the computer for hours at a time. That can't be good for you. All I do is slap a sticker on it and sell it. I'm telling you, you've got too much responsibility." She added with a decisive nod. "I'm going to start going with you when you go to the sales."

"And then who's going to run the store and put merchandise on the website? I can't do that. Other than looking stuff up, I'm no good with computers. You know that." She scowled. "You take care of the shipping, the advertising, all kinds of things I can't imagine doing. No. We have a good system going here. I will *NOT* be the reason for you to take on more work." She smoothed her long brown hair. "I'm fine." To prove the point, she sat up in bed and slung her legs over the edge. Then she winced. Her left hand went to her head again.

"Rachel, will you get Aunt Jane's medicine? It's in the medicine cabinet."

Going back to the bathroom, I tried to not look at Bretta's picture as I grabbed Aunt Jane's medicine. But I couldn't help it. There was something about the picture that bothered me.

"Did you find the medicine?" Mom called.

"I've got it," I said, hurrying back and handing it to Aunt Jane.

"This should work faster. It's one of my new ones." Swallowing the medicine, she looked at us. "You're both wonderful," she smiled. "My health is fine, Liz. It's these ridiculous dreams and headaches I can't get a handle on. I'm okay with the rest of it." She glanced at her right hand again and grimaced. "You know, at least when I'm dreaming, I'm still able to use that arm," she said, nodding at her right side.

I scooted Aunt Jane's slippers aside, and a memory flashed in my mind. I remembered why I was bothered by the picture of Bretta.

"I have to go to the bathroom. I'll be right back," I said. Closing the door, my gaze went to the picture. On Bretta's feet were pink shoes. She was always asking to borrow my shoes. Her mom bought shoes she hated so I let her borrow mine. Sometimes I got them back, and sometimes I didn't. I'd never get the last pair she borrowed. They were plaid and marked with her other personal effects somewhere in some sterile bag. I wondered if they found her vintage watches. She wore them everywhere, usually more than one. None of them worked, but she liked the way they looked.

Would they find out the shoes were mine? I'd never worn them, but Mom had seen them when I came home. As soon as she'd left, Bretta asked for them. She left a pair of pink sneakers in their place.

I looked nervously at the picture again. If the police found out, they would ask questions. I felt cold inside, but it had nothing to do with the temperature in the house. Opening the door, I heard Aunt Jane's voice.

"You didn't have to take me in, you know. You could have looked the other way. A lot of people would have."

"I didn't take you in, silly. You're my sister-in-law, and I love you like you were my own sister. I honestly don't know what we'd do without you. No more harebrained talk like that." When Mom looked at me and smiled, I noticed tiny worry lines around her eyes. When did she get those? "Rachel, you go on up and crawl in bed. I'll come and check on you in a minute, okay?"

I nodded and headed for the door. I pulled it shut but not completely. I was about to walk away when Aunt Jane's voice caught my attention. It wasn't so much her voice as it was her words.

"Our Rachel's a good girl, Liz. She's got a good head on her shoulders. She'll work through this."

"I know. I'm proud of her. She's had it pretty rough. What happened to Bretta hit her hard." I leaned forward to hear Mom's words.

"It would help if she had a father to lean on." Aunt Jane's voice was muffled. She must be pulling on her clean gown.

"She's got a father to lean on. He listens to her every day."

"I meant the kind of father who actually lives in the house and takes out the trash, Liz."

"I know what you mean, Jane."

"Do you still think about Steve?"

There was a long pause. "Every day." I heard sadness in Mom's voice.

"You think he'll ever come back, Liz? He might, you know, if I weren't here."

I knew I was spying on a private conversation but couldn't move a muscle. My worries about the police and their questions blew out of my head as I concentrated on the conversation between Mom and Aunt Jane.

"I think Steve will come back, Jane. And don't think like that. His absence has nothing to do with you."

"It has everything to do with me."

Another pause. Then a sigh. "I guess he'll come back when he's ready. Until then, there's not a whole lot we can do about it. For all I know, there's someone else in his life now. He stopped telling me he loved me a long time ago. San Diego seems to be his home right now, and I guess he likes it. He was never one to stay where he wasn't happy." There was an uncharacteristic edge to Mom's voice. "He still sends money every month to help with Rachel's clothes and household costs."

"Did he leave the force?"

"For a while. Then he decided to go back."

I'd never heard the two of them talk like this. They probably wouldn't be talking about him now if I were in the room with them. I knew about some of the stuff they were saying. I knew Dad sent money and that he was in San Diego, but what did the rest of it mean? What did Aunt Jane mean about it having everything to do with her? It didn't make sense.

I never understood why a grown man would leave his family, but I never felt like Aunt Jane was to blame. That was crazy. I was used to being a one-parent kid. I wasn't the only one out there. Other kids had dads who ditched them, too. Some mothers didn't stay around. Mom was right. We were doing okay, and Aunt Jane was a big part of why we were a stable family. I wanted to march back in there and say so, but her next words stopped me dead.

"If I hadn't been with him that night, everything would have been different."

"This is old ground, Jane. I've told you a million times. If you hadn't been with him that night, he'd probably be dead."

"But …"

"No buts. You know I'm right. Now lay back and let your medicine work."

I could tell Aunt Jane's words were slowing down. I heard the click of the bathroom light and decided I better hustle upstairs. I prayed Mom wouldn't hear me climbing the stairs.

I reached my room without making one old floorboard creak. I scrambled into bed, pulled the covers up under my chin, and shivered. The nights were almost always cold in Arkansas in March. Sometimes, we had snow, but tonight, my chill didn't come from the weather.

I heard Mom stop right outside my door and then heard her bedroom door open and close.

I clicked on the lamp beside my bed and picked up my journal and the old dictionary. Scanning the E pages, I looked for the perfect word. It didn't take long. The eight letters nearly sprang off the page at me. *Eeriness*: **Uncanny, so as to arouse superstitious fear; weird.**

Gripping my pen, I began to write.

Today is Tuesday. But just barely. 12:03 a.m. Aunt Jane had another nightmare and headache. I wish I had someone to talk to but there is—NO ONE—I can talk to. I want to talk to Bretta, but she's dead, and it's my fault. What I really wish is that I could turn time backward because then I could warn her—but that's not possible.

*There is an **eeriness** I've never felt. All the parents have gone crazy trying to make sure what happened to Bretta doesn't happen to their own kid. I feel so mad at myself and whoever made her die. Someone took Bretta's life away, and they sliced a part of mine away, too. They had no right.*

And now there's Mom and Aunt Jane. I don't get what they were talking about tonight. What happened to make Dad leave? And why does Aunt Jane say she's the reason? Mom says he lost his faith. Whatever. Bretta told me he didn't want to be tied down with a wife and kid. I was so furious with her for saying that.

Too much is happening. My head wants to explode and all I want to do is hole up somewhere until things are back to normal. Normal????? Help me.

I put the journal under my covers, too tired to walk it back to my desk, and then I slid the dictionary back in its place on the shelf. Turning off the light, I slumped against my pillow and closed my eyes. I felt better after putting my thoughts on the paper. I've always liked journaling, but now I *needed* it. It made things more clear in my head.

Closing my eyes, I tried hard to pray.

Blank.

I never have been good at pretty prayers. They either came out sounding lame or rehearsed. I opened my eyes and looked at the little nightlight across the room. It's one of those old ones that turns and casts tiny stars across the ceiling. Sighing, I reached for my journal again and then stopped. I just wrote everything that was in my heart into my journal. Wasn't that what praying was all about? Telling God what was in our hearts? Asking His guidance? Everything in my heart that I wanted to share with God was right there on the page. Journal praying. That I could totally do.

For the first time in three days, I smiled.

And relaxed.

Punching up my pillows, I lay awake and watched the stars scatter across the ceiling. I thought about the conversation between Mom and Aunt Jane. Dad's face floated up. The pictures around the house, the few that Mom still had out, showed a dark-haired man with muscles. He was tall with a great smile. He wasn't bad looking. In fact, for a man his age, he looked okay. So what made him so unhappy that he pulled out of the whole family plan? Maybe it was like Bretta said. He wanted his freedom, but ....

Was he selfish? Was I becoming like him? Had he really left because he didn't want to be around a sister who had a paralyzed arm and a wife and kid who needed him? Was he afraid we would all need him too much?

Nothing made sense. Too much had happened in one week – in one day. I felt overwhelmed again. My mind wouldn't stop cranking. What had Mom meant when she said he could have been killed in the accident? Why would that have anything to do with him leaving us? *Why* had he left?

I tried to remember exactly what had happened six years ago. That was when Aunt Jane came to live with us. We'd all been together then. They told me she was in a wreck and couldn't use her right hand. She moved in with us, so we could all help each other.

Dad was on the local police force then, and he remodeled our old house to include a new bedroom and bath especially designed for Aunt Jane. Helping him had been fun. I remember helping paint the room yellow, and Mom making new curtains. Dad worked long hours on the lighting and plumbing, and her room turned out great. They even let me paint a little daisy by the mirror in Aunt Jane's bathroom. Mom loved it. Even Dad had smiled and patted me on the head. The tiny flower was still there. It was right below the picture of Bretta.

Then Dad faded from the picture. He spent a lot less time at home. I remember asking Mom why he was always late. For a long time, she told me he had to work extra hours. Then he hadn't come home at all. Even at eight years old, I knew he didn't work twenty-four hours a day.

Six years was a long time. That was about the time Bretta had moved here from Missouri. Exit Dad. Enter Bretta.

Desolate. Now two people I cared about weren't in my life. I turned on my side and watched the nightlight stars again. It was a little bit like an old friend sitting there in the dark. The stars chased away shadows in my head, but something was still tugging at my brain; I couldn't put my finger on it. My eyelids began to droop. Glancing over at the clock, I realized I wouldn't get much sleep tonight. I nestled under the covers and was almost asleep when my mind clicked.

Aunt Jane said she'd been with him.

Mom said he could have been killed.

Aunt Jane had been in a horrible accident.

I sat up in bed, my heart pounding.

… And Dad had been the driver.

FOUR

*W*hen I woke up, I felt a tiny bit dazed. Figuring out what had happened between Dad and Aunt Jane made my mind reel. Why hadn't I figured this out before?

For a long time, I listened to house sounds. It was like rereading a really good book. I knew what all the characters were going to say and how I would react. But it was okay, because I liked the characters and what they said. Or at least I did most of the time.

We've lived in the same house all my life, so I knew exactly what each sound said. But this morning some of the sounds were missing. The house was way too quiet. By now, I should hear Mom and Aunt Jane talking downstairs. I shoved the covers back and heard my journal thunk to the carpet. The floor made my feet tingle from the cold, so I slid my feet into the slippers by my bed. These were Dad's old slippers. I stood there for a minute, looking at them. Then I kicked them off. Padding over to my dresser, I yanked open my sock drawer and dug out a pair of woolies. Remembering my journal, I grabbed it from the floor and stuck it in my desk drawer.

I sneaked out and went to Mom's room. The door was shut, and I couldn't hear anything. Was she sleeping? Maybe she'd never gone to sleep but had decided to go back to sit in Aunt Jane's room instead.

I started to the kitchen to check the calendar on the fridge. Aunt

Jane always marked which sales she planned to go to and the time they started. I was halfway down when I realized there was another sound missing. Edna wasn't scooting her food dish around. When I got to the kitchen, I glanced at the clock. It was 6:45. She always started nudging around 6:00.

Walking around the kitchen, I searched all her usual napping spots. Our old house had lots of hidey holes, and Edna loved all of them. She especially liked to sleep in the tiny broom closet. I guessed snoozing on top of a box of dusting rags was very gratifying to a cat.

But this morning she wasn't there. I couldn't find her anywhere, and I was beginning to worry when I heard a loud purr come from the laundry room.

Didn't want to think about Dad. I shoved him right out and followed the purring sound. When I flipped on the light, there sat Edna, curled on top of yesterday's clean clothes. She squinted at the blaring light and yawned. She gave me one of her looks that told me I was rude and thoughtless. Then, realizing one of her meals was late, she jumped out of the basket and ran to her food bowl.

She stopped and glared at me when she reached the empty container. I smiled and went to the cabinet, pulled out her food, and poured some into her bowl. "There you are, Princess Edna," I said, petting her gray fur.

Tugging the toaster out of the corner cabinet, I stuck some bread into the slots and punched the lever down. I still had a few minutes before I had to go upstairs and get ready for school.

School. I didn't want to think about going. All the kids would act even stranger since the assembly yesterday.

I remembered the reason I came down in the first place. I went to the refrigerator to check Aunt Jane's schedule for the day. Maybe if she had a sale to go to, I could fill in for her. I knew I wasn't old enough to bid at auctions, but I could handle an indoor rummage sale. I knew the kind of stuff she and Mom liked to sell in their shop and online. I didn't like to admit it to anyone, but I sort of liked old stuff. Yeah, I could definitely handle a rummage sale today.

Plus, it would be great not to have to go to school. Just this once. I was out of luck, though, when I scanned the calendar, nothing was marked. Apparently, Aunt Jane planned to do something else today. I turned back to the toaster and took out my breakfast. It didn't look very good. I put it in a saucer and set it beside the sink. Mom might eat it when she came down. I started back up the stairs to get dressed. No use putting it off. I had to go to school.

Thirty minutes later I was dressed and back in the kitchen. Edna had finished her breakfast, and Mom was standing at the stove stirring oatmeal.

She had a big smile on her face. "Ready for some real food? I found that pitiful bagel. I'm fixing you something hot. It's chilly this morning. According to the outside thermometer, it's 52 degrees."

"That's okay. I'm not very hungry. I've gotta go, or I'll be late for first period, and you know who I have first period."

"I'm driving you this morning, so you have plenty of time to eat something first."

"You don't have to do that, Mom. It's only a fifteen-minute walk. I love to walk. You know that."

"I know. And you know I worry about you." She turned around and poured hot oatmeal into a bowl. That was her signal that the conversation was over. I sat back in my chair. Was this new routine going to go on until I graduated? Sooner or later, things would calm down again. Wouldn't they?

Mom set the steaming bowl in front of me and brought the butter dish and cinnamon and sugar shaker over. She always fixed this when she was trying to cheer me up. But this time, oatmeal wouldn't fix things. Some pieces are too tiny to glue back together.

Mom busied herself around the kitchen and then went to check on Aunt Jane. "She's still asleep," she said, tiptoeing into the kitchen. "Bless her heart. I'm going to let her sleep as long as she can this morning." She glanced at the calendar to check the same thing I checked earlier.

31

"She doesn't have any sales," I said, around a mouthful of oatmeal.

"Good. She can rest today. I'll fix something and leave it for her before I go to the shop. I'll check on her at noon when I come home."

"I don't guess you'd like some help in the store, would you?" I asked.

She stopped washing the dish she was working on and turned to look at me. "Honey, you don't have to go to school today if you don't want to. I know yesterday was hard for you. I probably shouldn't have sent you, but I didn't know what to do. I was afraid if I didn't – well, you know. I guess I thought going would keep your mind occupied."

The worry on her face made me change my mind. "I'm fine, Mom. I just hate having Mrs. Bentley first period. It's not a great way to start the day. I think she really hates me."

"I doubt that. You've never had a teacher who didn't like you, Rachel. But, still, if you aren't up to going …"

I was acting like a spoiled, whiney little kid. "No. I'm fine." I hesitated. "I miss Bretta," I said quietly.

"I know, honey. They're going to find who did this."

My spoon clattered to the floor, and I bent to pick it up. "I have to go get my backpack. I'll be right back." Leaving my bowl and breakfast things on the table, I went upstairs to get my stuff. I made sure the newspaper was still inside. I knew Mom wouldn't search my room, but I didn't want to take any chances. If she saw the newspaper, she might start putting two and two together.

***

Thirty minutes later, she was dropping me off in front of a very big crowd of kids. Five duty teachers stood in front of the school. Normally there were two. When we pulled up, all five teachers and most of the kids moved to the far side of the building. It was like they had practiced what to do. For about two seconds, I stared at the swarm of people. Then I saw the reason they moved.

In huge letters, someone had written, "Goodbye, Bretta."

I think I forgot to breathe. I also forgot to shut the door to the car.

I realized Mom was saying something to me.

"Are you okay? Do you want to go back home? Rachel, answer me." Her voice was getting high and squeaky like it does sometimes when something has broken around the house, and she can't figure out how to fix it. I turned around and gave her a smile. She looked relieved and smiled back, but the way she crept forward in the car line told me she was watching as I walked toward the banner. I couldn't take my eyes off it. Bretta's name was in such huge letters—each one was red. The banner looked vulgar to me. I reached out and touched the B. It was cold.

"Hey, Rachel." I whipped around and looked into Pam's face. She was the only one near. Everybody else had moved away, even the teachers.

"Hey," I replied.

"Do you like the banner?" Pam asked cautiously.

I tried to nod, but it just sort of stuck. "Someone went to a lot of trouble," I said.

"All of the girls' basketball team did it last night. We wanted to do something, and we didn't really know what to do, so …"

I turned back toward the huge sign. "Thoughtful. Bretta would have liked it." I was lying. Bretta would have hated it. The letters were all crooked, and some of the paint had run. Neat, obsessive Bretta would have sneered at it. I didn't tell Pam that.

"We called Mrs. Doyle and asked if it would be okay. She called Mr. Jennings, and he said it was, so we put it up early this morning. We wanted to have it up when, you know, when you got here. I was hoping— we all were hoping it might help some."

The hot tears from yesterday were close to spilling over. I was a jerk. Pam and the others worked hard to do something nice for me, and I almost blew it. I swallowed hard. "It's nice, Pam. Really. I appreciate it a lot. Bretta's parents will, too."

"Well, we took up a collection for flowers, too, but since we don't know when the service is going to be …" Pam shrugged.

"I know. Everything's on hold, I guess. Maybe we'll find out something today."

Pam smiled. "We've never been—like best friends or anything, Rachel, but if there's anything I can do to help, I'd like to try. I can't believe this has happened. Can you?"

I dropped my head, and I guess she misunderstood. She thought I was sad. It wasn't sadness that made me drop my head. It was guilt. "Oh, hey, Rachel, I'm sorry. I didn't mean to upset you. My mom says I'm always saying the wrong thing, you know. I guess maybe she's right. Well, if I can help, let me know." She hurried over to a group of girls. I'd probably hurt Pam's feelings, and that made me sick inside. I couldn't look in their direction.

Thank goodness I didn't have to. I started through the doors and was swallowed up in the rush of getting to lockers and homeroom.

By 8:15, I was sitting in my new seat in Mrs. Bentley's class, waiting for her to make her entrance. It didn't take long. This time, she didn't have a folder with her. The way she stood let all of us know she was in no mood for interruptions of any kind.

If I could make it through two more months with her, I'd never have to see or hear her again. That should have cheered me up. It didn't. The image of the banner was still plastered in my mind.

"Take out your notebooks and pencils," Mrs. Bentley ordered. Everyone snapped to attention, and the slap of notebooks on the desktops was loud. The room was filled with the tiny click-clicks of two dozen mechanical pencils. Andy Bells raised his hand.

"Yes, Andrew?" Mrs. Bentley asked with a frown.

"Does this have anything to do with the art contest? Cause if it does, I've already done mine. I decided to draw one of them weird pictures that don't look like nothin'. You wanna to see it?"

"No, it is not about the art contest, and no, I do not want to see it. I will share this with you, Andrew, and I sincerely hope you listen carefully and adjust your future use of the English language accordingly. If the grammar in your announcement is indicative of the effort in your art piece, your submission will be rejected." She turned away from a confused-looking Andy and continued.

"This writing prompt is a type of pre-writing assignment for you. It will serve two purposes. One: to ready you for the approaching exams. Two: to help you all reach some type of closure. I want each of you to write a two-page essay about Bretta Deevers."

There was a buzz that began in the back of the room and grew as kids turned to look at each other.

"Since this assignment is not to be completed with a partner, I see no reason for discussion among any of you." Her eyes scanned the room, and every voice hushed. Her gaze stopped when she looked at me. "I realize Bretta was a classmate, and something quite unfortunate has happened to her. It's my belief that writing is one of the most therapeutic tools we have. With that in mind, each of you will work on a two-page essay regarding your relationship with Bretta Deevers. The paper is due tomorrow. No exceptions. No extensions. Anyone choosing not to comply with this assignment will be issued a zero. Is that understood?" Every head nodded. She checked her watch. "You may begin writing now. You will be given twenty-five minutes of class time. Those of you who would like to use the computers in the back may do so, but you will not save your work on the computer. You may print it out, but you may not save it to a flash drive. Those of you who do not complete the assignment today will need to complete it this evening. After the twenty-five minutes, we will cover information from the handout you received yesterday. Do not forget on Friday you have a test to prepare for."

I could not believe this woman. How was I supposed to write two pages about Bretta? Didn't Mrs. Bentley understand this assignment would be torture? I looked around the room. Andy was still scratching his head, trying to figure out what Mrs. Bentley had said to him. Others were tapping their pencils on their jaws or making their way to the computers. Some were looking around the room for—what? Inspiration maybe. Why was she really giving this assignment? Did she think it would be "therapeutic," or did she just have some twisted, macabre sense of humor?

"Excuse me, Mrs. Bentley." I swiveled in my seat to look at Billy Isley.

"Yes, Billy. What is it?" The look on her face clearly showed that Mrs. Bentley did not like to be bothered after her explanation of the day's assignment. But Billy had only been at Seely for a few months and didn't understand that you just don't ask Mrs. Bentley a question unless you've got a death wish or you're really hard up for an answer. He was about to get his answer.

"Well, I didn't know Bretta very good. I'm not sure I can fill up two whole pages. That's a lot of space."

"Yeah. I mean, yes, ma'am. Billy's right," Andy said. "It's not like she was the friendliest person in the world." The whole room grew quiet. Some of the kids looked at the floor, but some of them, including Pam, looked at me. When Andy remembered I was in the room, his face turned red. I could tell he was wishing he could grab the words and cram them back in his mouth. I almost felt sorry for him, and then I noticed several kids were nodding.

"Bretta was unique," Mrs. Bentley said. "She was bright and vibrant. Perhaps she didn't always conform to what each of you would have her do, but the fact remains that she is gone, and I believe her death will have a dramatic impact on each of you. I want you to explore your feelings not only about Bretta and her death but also about what she *could* have been. Sadly, we'll never know." She turned to stare at me. "Perhaps that is the most tragic part of an untimely death. Those left behind must ponder what could have been."

My stare held hers. She knew something.

FIVE

I managed to scribble for twenty-five minute and was relieved when Mrs. Bentley didn't ask for our pre-writing. I think she would have been a little surprised to see what I'd written. Even I was surprised. It had nothing to do with Bretta. It had a lot to do with Mrs. Bentley. But the woman was right. I did find it therapeutic.

My writing wasn't the kind of thing my pastor would find any humor in. Ashamed, I walked out of the room and shredded it.

My mind was churning.

Was it possible I hadn't seen Bretta the way other people saw her? At least half the class nodded when Andy spoke up about her not being friendly. I never really stopped to think about it. Now I did. Up until a month ago, I couldn't remember Bretta having other friends. I knew she was always mad at me when I talked about doing things with other people, but I'd been kind of flattered she wanted my friendship exclusively. Now, I was starting to see that a lot of these people thought Bretta was a snob. For the last month, she even ignored me.

I wasn't going to think about that.

I hurried into the hall during the ten-minute break before second period began. I realized I was thirsty and headed toward the vending machines by Mrs. Bentley's room. We weren't allowed to take anything into our classrooms, but we could buy juice or water and keep it in our locker. Harvey was filling the last machine in line.

He looked up and smiled at me. He was shy, always ducking his head when a crowd of kids was around. He looked around Mom's age and always looked sad. He reminded me of a basset hound. Even his ears drooped. He'd been taking care of the vending machines forever and was a regular on campus.

"Morning, Harvey." I smiled. I handed my money to him, and he handed me a bottle of peach juice.

"How do you remember what everybody drinks?" I asked.

"I don't," he chuckled. "You're the only one who gets the peach juice." He made a face.

"I can't be the only one. It's always empty, and I only buy a couple a week."

"Maybe there are other people out there, *somewhere,* who like the taste of peach pits."

"Nasty," I said. "Maybe it's time to try something else." I started to walk away but stopped at his next words.

"You know, my brother died when he was ten. I know how hard it is to lose somebody. I'm sorry to hear about your friend."

I didn't know what to say. I just stood there until Andy from first period hurried up to get something to drink. Harvey reached in and grabbed an apple juice for him. Andy smiled, saluted, and handed over his money. I watched as he disappeared around the corner. He was headed to Mr. Keely's class. I started toward history, but about halfway down the hall, I turned around. I realized Harvey might think I was being rude if I didn't reply. I didn't want him mad at me.

"Thanks, Harvey." I said. He nodded his head. I was glad I stopped to thank him. Bretta's death was horrible. I can't imagine what it would be like to have a family member die. Maybe that was why I was so protective of Aunt Jane.

***

It's probably a good thing Tuesdays are set aside for what Mr. Peterson calls independent study. I didn't think I could take notes about history if he decided to lecture. I pulled out my copy of *The*

Diary of Five Teenagers while some of the kids went to the laptops to search the databases for more information about Hitler's reign. We were studying the Holocaust and usually, I had a hard time putting the book about the teenagers down. It was the story of five who survived Hitler's gas chambers. But today, the book couldn't hold my attention. I must have read the same paragraph at least ten times.

My mind kept skipping back to Mrs. Bentley's assignment. I knew I had to turn in a paper tomorrow. It shouldn't be that hard to sit down and write two pages about Bretta. But it was. I knew her better than anyone else... Maybe that was the problem. I would have to be careful with the words I chose to describe her. And myself. I didn't intend to give anything away.

When the day finally ended, the jumble of cars waiting outside didn't surprise me and chaos was definitely on the low side. The same patrol car I saw yesterday had everyone in a line. The teachers had all students at the entrance and wouldn't let any of us near the curb until our ride pulled up. So, one at a time, we filled the cars and headed home. Mom was still looking tired, but she tried to throw a high-wattage smile my way when I flopped into the front seat.

"Hey. How're you doing?"

"I'm fine, Mom." Slinging my backpack to the floorboard, I fastened my seat belt and settled in for the ride home. Mom was big into seat belts. She usually refused to put her foot on the gas unless my belt was fastened. Knowing about Dad and Aunt Jane, I understood her obsession a little better. "Was it any better today with Mrs. Bentley?" I guess I jumped at the mention of her name because Mom looked alarmed.

"Honey, do I need to talk to her? I'll be happy to turn the car around right now and go speak to the woman." That was the last thing I needed!

"No, Mom. Everything is fine. I'm a little freaked out about the way the day started. You know, the banner thing. It caught me off guard. That's all. My classes went fine," I lied. I didn't mention the writing assignment to her. I was afraid she'd want to read it.

"Did you find out who was responsible for the sign?"

"Yeah, the girls' basketball team did it. Pam Nichols said they also took up money for flowers, but they did the banner for her folks— and for me."

She was quiet for a moment. "That was a nice thing for them to do, Rachel. They must care about you."

"I used to be friends with a lot of them when we were little kids. It was nice." I tried to remember when I stopped being friends with them. I played with most of them when I was little. Then I hadn't. Bretta had moved here. Andy's comment about Bretta started a snowball rolling inside my head. I was ready for it to melt and go away.

I didn't say that to Mom.

When we got home, I carried my backpack to my room and put it by the computer. The monitor teased me. It was like Bretta was still sitting there, pleading with me.

I knew I had to use it tonight to do my report, but for now, I turned my back and went downstairs to find Aunt Jane. She was sitting in the den reading a book about old dishes. She looked up and winked.

"Hi. I didn't hear you come in. Come sit by me. I think I might have a hug for you." I sat on her left side. Sure enough, she squeezed me in a tight hug.

"You don't have on that glow-in-the-dark orange lipstick, do you?" I grinned.

"No, I threw that away when it didn't work on Mr. Denning. I thought that would really turn him on." She shook her head. "It didn't."

I laughed. "You should have rubbed frosting behind your ear. From the looks of him, that would have worked better."

"You're probably right. I may try that next time."

Mom came into the room and stood in front of the fire. "We sold three pieces of furniture today, ladies." I pumped my arm and fist, and

Aunt Jane whistled. Evidently, her head was a lot better. I was glad.

"Which three?" she asked.

"A cabinet, a trunk, and a retro chair. They were all pieces *you* found last month. I would have sworn we'd be stuck with that trunk till the cows came home, but the buyer didn't even argue. She paid full price and smiled while she was putting it on her credit card. She said she'd been looking for one like that forever."

Aunt Jane blew on her fingernails and pretended to polish them on her lapel. "What can I say? I'm good." She smiled and held up the book she was reading. "It seems the dishes that were in that old cabinet we bought at the last auction are very old, very ugly, very rare, dishes. We can charge a fortune for them and probably get it. I'm telling you now. I expect a steak dinner out of this."

Mom's mouth was hanging open, and I laughed again. She almost never looked astounded. "How much are we talking here?" she asked.

"Oh, at least a couple of thousand," Aunt Jane replied calmly. Mom sank down on a pillow.

I left the two of them to discuss ugly plates and dinner. It was Mom's night to pick so I knew to expect BBQ meatballs. Tomorrow night, Wednesday, was my night. That meant cheeseburgers and curly fries. Thursday was mish-mash leftovers. Friday and Saturday were treat nights. We'd either go out for a pizza or order something in. I guess the routine was predictable, but I was beginning to think maybe predictable wasn't a bad thing. On Sunday, we all got in the kitchen and cooked dinner together and always fixed something brand new. Sometimes it turned out great. Sometimes not. But we had a good time.

I found Edna hiding on a kitchen chair so I picked her up and carried her upstairs. I didn't want to leave my homework until the last minute. I'd do math and history and then work on the essay. That was going to be the hardest. The other stuff I could do in thirty minutes.

Sitting on the bed, I held Edna and petted her. She loved the attention and turned into a purr machine. I stopped long enough to dig my history and math homework out of my bag and carried them and

Edna back to the bed. Twenty minutes later I was finished. Sighing, I stared at the computer. I decided to write my first draft of the essay in longhand. I wanted to put off typing it as long as I could.

I went to my desk and pulled out an extra notebook. Edna curled up on my pillow while I plopped in my beanbag in the corner. I looked at the computer. I imagined Bretta sitting there, tapping at the keys and giggling. She came home with me for hot dogs, and we brought them up to my room. I spilled mustard on my jeans and went to the bathroom to wipe off the stain. When I came back, I peeked over her shoulder.

"You're in a chat room!" I exclaimed.

"Shh. Would you be quiet? Your mom is going to hear."

"I'm not allowed to go into chat rooms. Neither are you. Are you crazy?" I asked.

"That's why I'm doing it here. She rolled her eyes. If my mom found out I've been chatting, she'd ground me for a month."

"And you think I won't get in trouble?"

"Your mom thinks you're perfect. Mine knows better. That's why I don't do it on my computer. I use my phone."

"I thought your mom wouldn't get you a phone…."

"She didn't. IB did. *That's* the kind of friend she is, Rachel. A generous one."

"Somebody bought you a phone!"

"Yes. Why are you surprised? When I told her I had to sneak around and use the computer at the coffee shop to get into a chat room, she sent a brand-new phone to me. She even paid for the service. They're rich!" she squealed. "Her parents are like doctors or something. It's great. Now I can do what I want online, and my mom doesn't have a clue!"

"So why aren't you doing this on your phone?" I asked.

"Because it's dead," she said, pulling the phone from her pocket. "Can I charge it? It's the same kind as yours. Takes the same kind of cord." She popped out of her seat and plugged it into the charger in my walk-in closet without waiting for me to answer. I waited while she took her time plugging it in. Then I heard her punching the keys and then a ping like she'd sent a message to somebody.

"How long have you been chatting?"

"About a month. But I've only had the phone for a week, and I've still got to get a charger and cord."

"Who is IB?"

"Someone who understands me." She smirked. "She likes to do the same things as me, and *she* is so funny. I found her in an art chat room."

"How old is she," I'd asked.

"Sixteen. We have a lot in common, Rachel. I've always been way more mature. Plus, she's from the west coast, and you know how I feel about California."

I did. Bretta was always telling anyone who would listen how she'd love to live there. "You don't know anything about her. How do you know she's not mental? How do you know it's even a girl? You haven't given personal information, have you?"

Bretta had given me one of those "you're not my keeper" looks. "I happen to be perceptive, Rachel. I could tell by our texts if she wasn't being sincere. *She* is the most sincere person I've ever met."

That stung. "Don't you get it, Bretta? This could be dangerous. And I don't get why you want to take that chance. This is serious. I would never do that."

"No. You wouldn't. I'm not afraid of taking chances, Rachel. Like I said. I'm way more mature. That's why I'm meeting her tomorrow."

I must have looked totally spaced because she laughed. "Anyway, she'll be in town, which makes it the perfect time. Her folks are coming to a convention in Little Rock, and they're bringing her with them just so she can meet me. They're going to bring her to the park. Cool, huh."

"And your parents are okay with this?" Bretta hesitated and turned back to the laptop, twirling that long, blonde hair. When she didn't answer, my stomach started knotting up.

"My parents don't know about it." Then she turned to look at me.

"I need you to help me out," she pleaded. "I'm going to tell them I'm going to the mall. They won't even question that. But instead of going there, I'm going to meet IB. You'll cover for me, won't you? You know, in case they call. They probably won't even bother, but in case they do, I need you to tell them I'm at the mall."

"No. This doesn't feel right," I said.

"I'd do it for you."

"But I wouldn't ask you to."

"I've done other stuff for you, Rachel. You owe me."

She was right. She had done favors for me. But letting me borrow notes or clothes wasn't the same thing as asking me to lie. "I don't know, Bretta."

"Fine. I knew you weren't really a friend. I knew I couldn't count on you when I needed you." She'd spat the words out, and I knew she was mad. And she was mad *at me*. I'd looked at the computer and then at the back of her head. She was sitting yardstick straight.

"Have you even had a real conversation with her?"

"No, but I will tomorrow."

"Bretta, look at it from my side."

"I don't have to! You're an immature, selfish baby who is way too sheltered and always trying to act holier than the rest of us. I'm sick of it. You only think of yourself, Rachel. IB's parents have gone to a lot of trouble to make this happen."

Maybe she was right. I was sheltered. She wasn't the first person to tell me my faith set me apart. The last thing I wanted was to look like a fool. I hung my head and paced across the room. "Okay, Bretta. I'll do it."

She'd turned around with a smile on her face. She had known all along I would do anything to keep her from being mad at me.

"Awesome." She began typing again. Then she'd hit one final button.

That was the last time I saw her. She left an hour later with three things. A promise from me I wouldn't tell anybody about her meeting, and my new pair of shoes … plaid ones, size six. That's why I didn't want Mom to see the newspaper picture. She might figure out the shoes were mine, and that might raise questions.

Yeah, it was going to be hard to write a paper about Bretta. Mainly because I was the only one who knew she set up a meeting in the park with a stranger. And then she was murdered. She died because I kept my mouth shut.

SIX

*S*ince Bretta's death, I've been crazy, worrying someone was going to figure out I had been involved.

My visit with Mrs. Doyle on Monday was almost a disaster. I still looked over my shoulder for the police to pop up any minute—until today. In today's paper, which I found in the school library, one of the detectives said they now believed her murder was a "random act of violence," committed by somebody passing through town. If they only knew just how close to the truth that was. It was eating me up not to tell somebody about her meeting with this IB person, but if I did, I was sure to land in a huge pile of trouble. Bretta had been my friend, and I let her down. I gave in and put her in danger. If I had told her no, she might be alive.

I stared at the words on the laptop. I finished Mrs. Bentley's assignment. It was titled simply: Bretta. Punching the print icon, I watched it spit out exactly two pages.

"Rachel," Mom yelled up the stairs. "Dinner's ready." I slid the papers into my binder and stuck it in my backpack along with the math and history homework. I looked at my clock. 6:32.

"I'm coming," I yelled back. Turning off the computer, I looked around the room and half expected to see Bretta standing there. My mind had been so focused on her for the last hour I felt like she was there in the room with me.

I went downstairs.

"Here," Aunt Jane said, as she tossed a towel. "Grab the rolls out of the oven. I'll get the butter."

Eating was not big on my list of things to do right now. But if I didn't eat, they would make it into a big deal. Mom was dumping the meatballs into the sauce and giving them their final stir. "Is there a salad?" I asked.

"Yep. It's in the fridge. Will you grab the dressing, too?" she asked. I went to the refrigerator, snatched up the salad and dressing and went back for the rolls. Thoughts of Bretta pounded around inside my head as I put the hot bread on the scuffed up old oak table.

The table had been one of Aunt Jane's finds at an estate sale. She and Mom had fallen in love with it and couldn't bear to sell it. Its old claw feet were huge. Edna loved to curl up in the niche of one of the feet and wait for goodies to be sneaked to her during meals. As we all gathered around the table, Edna assumed her favorite position.

Mom lit the candle in the middle of the table, and I smiled. She was a fanatic about candles. If Mom was around, a candle was lit somewhere.

A memory of Dad popped into my head. The fire alarm went off downstairs, and Dad went racing down the stairs, grabbing the extinguisher from its hallway hook. We could hear him fussing about how he'd known those candles would burn our house down. Mom and I were right behind him. When we got to the kitchen, it wasn't Mom's candles that had set off the alarm, but one of his cigarettes. The smoldering butt had caught a nearby dishcloth on fire. He never mentioned Mom's candles again. Right after that, he quit smoking.

Aunt Jane plopped the butter dish onto the table and patted my shoulder on her way to her chair. We settled around the table, and Aunt Jane said grace.

"How do you feel tonight, Aunt Jane?" I asked.

"Great. I've got an estate sale lined up for next week. It's in Little Rock, so I may go down the night before so I don't have to get up at the crack of dawn." Glancing at Mom I caught her smiling. I guessed it was about the expensive dishes Aunt Jane had found for a bargain.

"Are you taking the trailer?" Mom asked. Their trailer was a pooped-out old delivery van that had belonged to one of the local furniture dealers. Mom bought it for next to nothing when she and Aunt Jane started their business. It was really ugly, but it still ran. Aunt Jane was a master at handling the thing, but loading her purchases was a problem. With only one arm that worked, she had to have someone load the heavy pieces for her, and always took extra money to offer helpers.

"I think I better, Lizzie. You don't need it, do you?" she asked anxiously. "I didn't think to ask."

"No. It's just that I had a strange call from the police this afternoon wanting to know if we used it last Saturday," Mom said. I froze.

"Why on earth would they want to know that?" Aunt Jane asked. "It's always parked at the shop unless one of us is driving it. I didn't use it Saturday. Did you?"

"No," Mom said, shaking her head. "But evidently someone noticed a van parked near the exit of the park. The police are checking out all the local vans. Who knows? It may not have even been a van. It could have been a mini bus full of kids needing to get a drink or go to the bathroom."

My mouth felt dry. A van. Had the murderer been driving a van? "Did the witness notice the license plate?" I asked. "Were they out-of-state?"

"I don't know," Mom shrugged. "They didn't say who reported it, but I admire the police for investigating all their leads. What made you ask if they were out-of-state tags?"

I pretended to be studying my food. "I don't know. Guess I've been watching cop shows." If Mom noticed anything strange about my answer, she didn't let on.

"They just have to catch whoever did this." She paused as she chewed a meatball. "Which brings me to something important. Until this whole thing is over, I'll be taking you to school." She held up her hand when I opened my mouth. "No arguments, Rachel. I'm not taking any chances. If I can't take you, Aunt Jane will. Same thing goes for the afternoons. It won't hurt to close the shop a few minutes early to get you. I can always open up when I get you home."

"But Mom …" I started.

"No argument. Once you're here, you aren't to go out unless one of us knows where you are going and who you're with. I don't want you to open the door to anyone you don't know. Understood?"

"Yes, Ma'am. I understand."

"You're mama isn't trying to be hard on you," Aunt Jane said, patting my hand. It's— well, you're all we've got. We don't want anything to happen to you. Try not to be mad at a couple of overprotective old ladies. Okay?"

I nodded. I understood exactly what they were saying, but part of me felt like a prisoner. All of a sudden I felt the same as I had at school. I was mad that I in the middle of something I helped make and even madder that I couldn't do anything about it.

After dinner was over, I washed the dishes and tidied the kitchen. Mom went to work on her computer, and Aunt Jane went back to her book about the dishes. Even Edna had her own plan. She was sitting on her paws facing the hot water heater. This usually meant she heard tiny mouse feet. She could be there for hours.

The minute Mom mentioned the news about the van, my mind started forming an idea. Twice I pushed it away, but my thoughts wouldn't go away. I needed to go somewhere quiet and think about it, but I didn't really want to go to my room.

Instead, I went to the book closet. When Dad remodeled the house, this had been the big walk-in closet on the bottom floor. Mom had always loved books and had a ton of them, so he turned the closet into a mini library where she could stash her collection. He bought a set of beautiful brass bookends to give her the day he finished. She'd been so happy. I shrugged. Those days were over.

Still, the room was nice. He did a good job. It had a pocket door that gave me privacy. The bad thing was there wasn't any heat or air, so the little room was either stuffy or freezing, depending on the weather. Mom stopped using it after Dad left, so I started putting my own books on the shelves. This was my cozy place to hang out. Edna had her nooks. I had mine.

I curled up in the old leather chair, another of Aunt Jane's finds, and switched on the lamp. I was kind of surprised to find an open book lying beside the chair. It was a romance, so Mom must have left the book. She loved romantic books, but it surprised me she was using this room again. I scooted the book over.

The telephone rang. I heard Mom talking and then there was a knock on the pocket door.

"Rachel," she said, sliding the door open.

"Yeah, Mom. What is it?" I asked.

"That was Mrs. Deevers. Bretta's service is scheduled for Friday. She wanted to let you know before it's formally announced. There's also a box of stuff she wants to bring over. She said they were things that belong to you. I told her we'd be happy to pick them up, but she said she wanted to deliver them herself. Is there anything of Bretta's that you have? If there is, I could give it to her." She looked at her watch. "She said they'd be by in about fifteen minutes."

My mind was racing. I still had Bretta's old shoes. She wanted to wear my new ones home on Friday, and I let her. She left her old ones because she didn't want to carry them home. If I handed them over now, her parents might start to think about the ones she had on when she died. That would lead to questions about when she borrowed them, and that could lead to what she asked me to do.

I made up my mind. "No. I don't have anything. I did have her flash drive, but I gave it to Mrs. Doyle to take to Bretta's family." Mom hesitated. She was good at reading my eyes. I put my head down and pretended to look for a book.

"Okay. Well, I'll call you when she gets here. If you think of anything, run upstairs and get it. I know she'll treasure all of Bretta's belongings. It would mean a great deal to her to get all of them back."

I nodded and said I'd go upstairs and look again. I followed her into the hallway and started up the stairs. There was a pouncing sound in the kitchen, then a squeak. Edna had caught her mouse.

The first thing I did when I reached my room was hide Bretta's shoes. I stuck them in the back of my closet inside the shoebox my new shoes had come in. Then I put an old quilt on top of them, looking around the room for anything else of Bretta's. There was one thing. She sketched a picture for my last birthday. It was an angel. Her hair was brown, long, and flowing. The angel was hovering over a shorter, blonde girl. In fancy script, she labeled the angel as me and the girl as herself. She taped the charcoal pencil she used to sketch it under her name. The picture was taped to the wall. I didn't want to give that back. It was a birthday present. I wondered if she had started on my birthday present for this year. I'd never know.

"I didn't find anything, Mom," I lied. It surprised me how easy that rolled off my tongue. Then I explained about the picture.

"I'm sure she'd want you to keep that. Thanks for looking." She seemed preoccupied. She was updating our web page with new merchandise. I wandered off toward the closet. I'd just pulled one leg under me when the doorbell rang. Aunt Jane answered it. I heard voices in the hallway. Maybe I wouldn't have to face Bretta's parents. I didn't want to.

"Rachel," Mom called. I closed my eyes and tried to get myself together. What am I supposed to say to these people? Their daughter is dead, and oh, by the way, it's my fault.

"Coming." I tried to sound normal, but even I could hear the stupid quiver in my voice. I stopped at the den door. I hadn't seen Mrs. Deevers for a month. This woman didn't look anything like the slick blonde who was always fussing over the way she looked. This woman was a stranger. Bretta's mom was not this messed up, miserable looking woman. But beside her stood Bretta's dad.

"Hello, Rachel," Mr. Deevers said, nodding. "I hope we're not bothering you folks, but we wanted you to have these things. They belong to you. I know how girls are about swapping things out, and …" the sentence died on his lips. He stared at his wife. She stared at me. Mom spoke up and broke the silence.

"This is thoughtful of you both. Come in." She took the box from Mr. Deever's hands and watched as he sort of led his wife to the sofa. She cocked her head slightly and sniffed. Then she smiled and sat on the couch. She looked like some kind of stoned zombie.

"Did Bretta ever sit here?" she asked Mom.

Mom glanced at Mr. Deevers. He wiped his forehead and patted his wife on the shoulder.

"Oh, you know teenagers. They're all over the house," he said.

"Oh, my goodness, yes. Kids don't stay still for very long," Mom said, then rubbed at her arm. She always did that when she got nervous. "I'm so sorry about Bretta," she said. "If there's anything we can do, I hope you'll call on us. That's what friends are for."

I was still standing where I had been when they walked in the door. I took a deep breath and walked over to the coffee table. "I'm sorry." I said. "I miss her." Mrs. Deevers reached out and touched my hand. I didn't want her to touch me. Tears began sliding down her face. Her husband put his hand under her elbow.

"C'mon now. These folks are tired, and they need to get to bed. It's getting late. I'm sorry," he whispered to Mom. We could tell he wanted to say more, but he glanced at his wife.

Aunt Jane came over and led Mrs. Deevers to a painting on the other side of the room. I could hear her telling all about the local artist who had painted it. I watched Mrs. Deevers face light up as she told Aunt Jane that Bretta had been an artist.

I turned my back to them and went back to Mr. Deevers. He lowered his voice as he spoke to Mom and me. "I tried to tell her it wasn't necessary to do this right now, but she insisted. I'm at the end of my rope, Mrs. Reynolds. I've lost Bretta, and feel like I'm losing my wife, too. She's not eating, not sleeping. She roams through the house all night and day. She can't hold up like this."

"I think things will get better once Bretta's killer is caught," Mom answered. "At least then you'll have some closure. We're praying for you both, Mr. Deevers." Bretta's dad looked at her face for a long time. I think her words must have helped him because he nodded and seemed to relax.

"Thank you," he said. "I hope you're right." He looked over at his wife and made his way across the room. When he led her out the door, Aunt Jane closed it quietly behind them. No one said anything. We all stared at the door. Mom was the first to move.

She hugged me. "You okay?" she whispered in my ear.

"Yeah," I lied.

"Now do you understand why we don't want you walking to or from school?" I could still see the haunted look in Mrs. Deevers' face. I nodded into Mom's shoulder.

I lugged the box to my room and decided to take a shower. I couldn't go through these things right now. I needed some clear space in my head. The box would have to keep till tomorrow. I set it beside me on the floor and shoved it to the end of the bed. Stretching full out on the floor, the old wooden planks felt cold against my cheek. I tugged down the quilt from the foot of my bed to help with the chill from the floor. My energy was gone. I closed my eyes, sighed, and tried to wipe the day from my mind. It wouldn't go away.

I jerked awake and looked at the clock. 12:32 a.m. I took a deep breath and hugged the quilt, getting up slowly from the floor. Yawning, I stretched, reached for my dictionary then went to the desk to get my journal. I flipped to the F section and started searching. This time, I searched a long time to find a word. Partly because my mind was fuzzy with sleep and partly because it was late. I was tired of everything.

But when I finally did find the word, every inch of my arms tingled. Seven perfect letters. *Forlorn*: **Miserable in feeling. Hopeless. Alone.**

Wednesday a.m. 12:34

Today has been long. I can't believe Mrs. Bentley had us write an essay about Bretta. If there is a purpose to the assignment, except to torture us, I don't understand what it is.

Bretta's parents were here. I was in the closet library when they called. I wish I'd stayed there. They brought over a box of stuff I left at their house. They said they wanted me to have it. But I think there was another reason they came over.

Bretta's shoes are hidden away in my closet. They'll stay there. I don't want to give them back.

I wish her parents had stayed away. I didn't want to see Mrs. Deevers. She looked exactly the way I feel. **Forlorn.** *Even the sound of it on my tongue sounds sad. Yesterday I was mad, but today is different. I think I'd rather be mad. At least with that, you don't feel like hope is gone.*

I really want somebody to talk to. At least Mrs. Deevers has her husband. I can't tell anyone what happened. If I do, I'll get in trouble. I might even have to go to jail. What will that do to Mom and Aunt Jane? They'll be so disappointed in me. And what about Dad? How will he react when he finds out what I've done? Would he even care????

Sliding the dictionary back, I walked to the desk to tuck my journal away, tripping on the box. Frowning, I realized that, like Mrs. Bentley's assignment, it would be better to just go through the stuff now and get it over with. Plopping back down on the floor, I started digging in the box. There was a lot of junk. Stuff I forgot about having at Bretta's. How had her mom known they were mine?

But I knew the answer. Just like that. Bretta already had this stuff boxed up. There's no way her mom would know what stuff was mine and what was Bretta's. They didn't shop together. Bretta said they didn't even talk much except to fight. No. Bretta had a new friend, and the new Bretta would have wanted rid of the old Rachel— and all of the stuff that went along with her. My stuff.

Turning back to the box, my hand touched a notebook. It was one I loaned her. She'd been out sick, and I had taken notes for her. Lifting it out of the box, a small spiral notebook slipped from between the pages. Bending to pick it up, I realized this one wasn't mine. It had Billy Isley's name all over it. Billy from first period English. Why would Bretta have a notebook belonging to Billy? I opened it and began reading. The dates were from two months ago, right after he moved to town.

After fifteen minutes, I put the notebook on my desk. It was full of notes he and Bretta had written to each other. I wondered if there were more notes that might have something to do with Bretta. Those in front of me were pretty graphic. Sure didn't leave me wondering what kind of relationship they had. Apparently, they'd been meeting after school and on weekends. And they didn't meet to talk. The notes made that clear. Then she dumped him. Why hadn't she told me about Billy?

Another thought crossed my mind. Why would a guy who had been *very* friendly with Bretta tell a classroom full of people he didn't know her well enough to write two pages? What was he hiding?

SEVEN

The scream that ripped through the house brought me to my feet. But this time, I was the one screaming. I looked around. My heart was beating so hard I could actually hear it in my ears. Mom and Aunt Jane burst through the door and found me staring at the closet. I could have sworn I saw Bretta there.

"Rachel, are you all right?" Mom asked. She held onto me while Aunt Jane put her arm around my waist.

"She's shaking like a leaf," Aunt Jane declared. "C'mon, let's get you back in bed and under some covers." I let myself be tucked in. Glancing at the closet again, I remembered part of my dream. Already the images were beginning to fade. *Thank you, God*, I thought. I was pretty sure they wouldn't go away all together, but at least the really bad image of Bretta's bruised face wasn't floating in front of me now. Closing my eyes, I shivered. Aunt Jane went to get another quilt. She was headed toward my closet.

"Honey," Mom said. "What scared you? Was it a sound?"

"I was dreaming about Bretta." My voice quivered. I followed Aunt Jane's movements. Switching on the closet light, she struggled with the heavy quilt in the back of my closet. Mom went over to help her. She tugged it loose, and with it, several pairs of old shoe boxes. Bretta's shoes tumbled out on the floor. Mom tossed them back into the closet.

With a sigh of relief, I fell back onto my pillow. When I opened my eyes, Aunt Jane was giving me an odd look. Then it passed, and she was by my side, helping Mom smooth the quilt over the bed.

"It was too much," Mom said. "The visit from the Deevers, I mean. Sometimes I swear I don't have good sense. There's no way I should have put you through that. I could have taken the box and talked to them. I'm sorry."

"It's okay, Mom." I smiled. Usually, it was Aunt Jane's room we were all in late at night and her bed we were huddled around. If her nightmares were as bad as this one, I *really* felt sorry for her. My scare gave me a whole new appreciation for my aunt. How did she go through this on a regular basis?

"I'm sorry," I said, looking at both of them.   "What time is it?" I asked. Aunt Jane had switched off the closet light and it was too dark in the room to see the clock on the wall. The only light was from the hallway.

"It's a little after two," Mom said. "Honey, I've been thinking. Why don't you stay home and help me in the shop?"

I looked up excitedly and was on the brink of hugging her neck when I remembered Mrs. Bentley's assignment. If I didn't turn in the paper about Bretta, she'd give me a zero. Her words rang in my mind. No exceptions. No extensions. As tempting as Mom's offer was, I couldn't take a chance on getting an F on one of Bentley's assignments.

"Thanks, Mom," I said. "But I think I'd better go. I've got a huge test coming Friday, and I need the review." I looked down at the cover on my bed. I never felt more miserable. Something had to change. I glanced at the closet.

"Are you sure? I could call Mr. Jennings and explain."

"Or you could work with me. I could use the help," Aunt Jane chimed in.

I shook my head. "I'm okay," I said. Aunt Jane nodded and Mom searched my face. I'm not sure what she was looking for, but she sighed and stood.

"Okay. I'm leaving our doors open tonight, though. If you need me for anything, let me know, honey. I'll pray for you, sweetie." And she did. Right there. Three people. Six cold hands and a purring cat. I listened while Mom prayed for my peace of mind, my broken heart, and for a clear path.

"Amen," Aunt Jane said when Mom finished. "Now, I'm not quite as good as you are at getting that cloth just the right temperature, but I could practice. Your head isn't hurting, is it?" She asked quickly. I shook my head and snuggled down into the covers. Mom walked around the bed and switched on the nightlight. I was glad. It chased shadows away. I decided I liked that light.

I lay there for a long time, and a foggy idea from earlier formed into a good, solid decision in my head. I felt like a liar. I wasn't being honest with my family, and it was getting harder to hide the truth. Bretta's killer wasn't going to be caught unless I did something. And I owed it to her. Didn't I?

Turning over, I watched the nightlight while it turned and sent blue splashes of stars and constellations around my room. The dream had seemed so real. I felt like I was at the place where Bretta died. I saw her face, just before her attack and even felt her hand grab mine. It was a frantic grasp from someone who knew she was about to die. I saw her on the ground. Pale. Still. Stiff.

I drifted off, and the next thing I knew, the smell of bacon drifted through my room. The dead images from last night were replaced with resolve. I would do everything to find Bretta's killer. Then I would go to the police.

But I couldn't go to them without information. If I went now, they'd just brush me off as a drama teen. But if I went with the identity of Bretta's murderer, my efforts would be kind of like buying myself back. The truth would come out about my involvement but maybe her parents could forgive me for going along with their daughter's plan.

***

Ever since the murder, I began to wonder if the person she met really was a sixteen-year-old girl traveling with her parents. Bretta had been too trusting. I believed that whoever she met set her up. Anybody could have faked an identity that Bretta instantly related to. I didn't know who it was, but I knew I was going to find out.

I pulled my jeans on and tried to remember what she told me about IB. She was sixteen. What else had she said? Oh, yeah. Her new friend was sincere. That was the word Bretta had used. Sincere. And something else. The girl was from California. Or at least that's what she wanted Bretta to think. Who really knew?

But was it coincidence this person had said California was where she lived? Or did the person know enough about Bretta to know how interested she was in living there? She had been obsessed with living on the West Coast. She had already been making plans to go to the College of Arts in San Diego.

My stomach growled, and I pulled my sweatshirt over my head. After I straightened my bed, I headed down the stairs. For the first time in three days, I was genuinely hungry. I couldn't wait to get to the kitchen.

Usually through the week, we grabbed toast or cereal. But today, Mom got up early to fix a Sunday breakfast on Wednesday. She always cooked a lot when something went wrong. Yesterday oatmeal. Today bacon and eggs. I wasn't complaining. I glanced toward Aunt Jane's room and remembered she left early for a sale.

Outside, the rain was falling, and I was glad Mom was taking me to school. I didn't mind walking in a little drizzle, but this was a downpour. Edna was hiding in Aunt Jane's chair. That was her usual hiding place when there was thunder. During snowstorms, she curled up in the bathroom sink. Cats.

I went to the cabinet and pulled out two plates. The juice box sat on the table, so I poured a glass for myself and one for Mom. This morning her mind was somewhere else. She barely grunted when I kissed her cheek. I can tell when her mind is unscrambling a problem.

Sometimes she acted like this when she has a problem at the shop.

"Is everything okay at the store?" I asked.

"Everything's fine." She turned around and shoveled eggs into my plate. The bacon was on a dish to itself. She only fixed enough for one.

"Aren't you eating?" I asked.

"No. I'm not hungry this morning. I had a late night snack. Jane and I sat up and talked for a while."

"What's wrong, Mom?" What a lame question.

"Eat your breakfast, Rachel. It's getting cold."

"I'm not eating until you tell me what's going on. If you're worrying about me, I'm good. Last night things turned around. I made decisions after I woke up from that nightmare," I said. I wasn't about to tell her what they were, but I wanted her to know I was okay enough to solve my own problems. I thought it would put her mind at ease.

"I sent your father a text."

That got my attention. "Why did you do that?" I frowned.

"I told him about Bretta, and I told him about your nightmare last night, and," she sighed, "I told him I was worried about you."

"Why did you do that?" I demanded. "Dad doesn't care about my nightmares. He doesn't care about me! Period." Then I said something I shouldn't have. But I wanted to see her reaction. "I'm probably the reason he left." She looked at me sharply.

"That's not true, Rachel," she said. I hadn't seen that much fire in her eyes since I was ten and came home with a pet snake. "Your father loves you, and it's time you know that. I've been a little ... unwelcoming, I guess. I was hurt when he left."

"So why did you text him?" I sat back and crossed my arms. The look on her face should have made me apologize. Instead, I just shoved right on. "The three of us are doing fine. We don't need Dad to screw things up, Mom."

"He deserves to know what's going on, Rachel. He's your dad. It's not like he dropped off the face of the earth. We still hear from him every month."

"The only reason he sends money every month is for his conscience. It's not because he wants to help us out or because he wants to be a part of this family." I knew I was over the line, but I was mad. Those fuzzy feelings from ten minutes ago were gone. Inside me something started to burn. Did she think I was just some little kid? Why didn't she talk to me before she contacted Dad? I should have had a vote in this.

Mom flinched. "No. That's not true. He does care, Rachel. You were always the most important thing in the world to him. You still are."

I flopped back in the chair, appetite gone. "Okay. So tell me. What did this father who adores me say?"

"He hasn't answered yet, but I sent the message very early this morning after your— nightmare, so he probably hasn't seen it yet."

My mind was doing somersaults. "Did you tell Aunt Jane?"

"Yes. We agree it was the best thing to do. She thinks he needs to know what you're going through."

"And how exactly is he supposed to help? Mom, he hasn't seen me in six years. Six years! He probably wouldn't recognize me if I ran up and bit him. I'm not the little kid he walked out on, you know."

She stared at me. "Is that what you think? That he walked out on *you*?" She pushed her chair back and went to stand at the window. I could see her angry profile. "You need to understand there is a difference between walking out and walking away, Rachel. Your father didn't *walk out* on us. He walked away from us. Remember that." Her hands were clenched. So was her jaw.

Before I could open my mouth and ask her what that was supposed to mean, she left the room. Well, this was just great. I was finally getting control over myself again, and this happens. I sat and stared at the eggs. They looked like rubber. I shoved the chair back and took my plate to the trash. Dumping all the food into the plastic container, I slammed the door. Edna gave a sharp purr and stood up to look at me. Ignoring her, I put the plate in the sink and went back upstairs to get my backpack.

Mom was waiting at the door when I came down. I planned to ignore her earlier order about walking to school. Even in this downpour, I'd rather walk than have to breathe the same air as my mother. She would just try to tell me how I had the dad of the year. I'd have to listen to all of his good points. Well, I had news for her. I didn't want to hear them. She could save her breath.

As far as I was concerned, Bretta had been right. He got tired of us. Period. I hadn't seen him since I was eight. Six birthdays had gone by without getting so much as a hug. Six Christmases, I hurried down those stupid stairs, hoping to see him by the tree. He was the present I didn't get for six years. That was a long time. People could forget how to love somebody. He had. So had I.

I stomped to the car and climbed in, slamming the door. The ride to school was stone silent. Mom didn't say a word. Neither did I. The only sound was thunder. An occasional streak of lightning lit up the sky. Probably a sign about the way my day would be. When she pulled up to the drop-off site, I jumped out. No goodbye. I slammed the door and walked into the building.

I didn't go directly to Mrs. Bentley's room. Instead, I made a stop at my locker and then walked by Mrs. Doyle's office. Someone was talking to her, but she waved at me. I waved back. Maybe I could talk to her later about this whole Dad thing. That was a topic I felt totally safe discussing with her. She might even have some good advice. This sort of thing must come up all the time in a counselor's day. I slipped into the girl's bathroom to do something with my hair. When I was leaving, Pam Nichols came in.

"Rachel, hi. How are you?" she asked. She didn't seem nervous today. The smile on her face looked real enough.

"Pretty good. How are you?" I asked.

"Going crazy studying for Bentley's test." She rolled her eyes.

"Yeah," I agreed, although I hadn't spent any time studying for it yet.

"Why don't you come over after school today? Some of us hang out and study before a big test like this. You should come," she urged. "My mom's making pizzas. It'll be fun. If cramming for one of Bentley's tests can be fun."

I looked at Pam for a split second. "Sure. With everything going on, I haven't studied – at all."

She grinned and leaned over. "Me neither. But don't tell my mom. You want to ride home with me? I'm leaving right after school. We could meet at the front."

I hesitated for a whole half second. "Great," I said. "Thanks." I knew Mom would be at her computer from 8:00 to 9:00 before the shop opened. I hurried into the computer lab and sent her a quick e-mail telling her my plans. I didn't ask. I even told her she was welcome to call Pam's mother to check out my story if she wanted. Then I added a tacky p.s. and told her to be sure to let Dad know too.

I walked into first period and took off my jacket, barely glancing in the direction of Bretta's old desk. Pam smiled as I walked past and gave me a thumbs up.

I dug my essay out of my backpack and was smoothing it on my desk when Billy Isley walked into the room, "cocky" showing with every step. I stopped and watched while he slid into his seat and smiled at the girls around him. He messed with his hair. That was when I noticed it. There was a bandage on his hand.

He looked around the room and quickly stuck his hand in his jeans pocket.

The newspaper article said Bretta fought with her attacker. Had she scratched him? She could have. She had long nails. Now Billy had all my attention. I never really noticed him much before. But I did now. I looked at the way he was built. His arms were strong. They'd have to be for him to make it onto the wrestling team. He wasn't very tall, under six feet, but he was stocky. With short hair and a buffed body, he obviously thought he looked really hot. But everybody knew he was just a jock wannabe with no brain. What had Bretta liked about him? Was that why she hadn't wanted anyone to know about them?

Mrs. Bentley walked in and went to her desk. She wasted zero time in calling the class to order and getting down to business. "Class, please retrieve your essays. I'll be taking them up shortly. Um, let me see." She scanned the room. An idea clicked in my head. When she looked my way, I made eye contact with her— and smiled. "Yes, Rachel. Would you please pick up all the papers and deposit them on my desk?"

I couldn't believe my luck! Picking up my essay along with my notebook, I began making my way around the room getting everyone's reports. When I came to Billy, I studied him. He leered at me, looking me up and down. I stuck his paper on top of my notebook and made my way down the aisle. Pretty soon, I had everyone's assignment. I put them on Mrs. Bentley's desk. All but one.

I kept Billy Isley's. I was going to find out what he wrote about Bretta.

EIGHT

I stuffed my notebook and Billy's essay into my backpack. I held my breath to see if Bentley reached for the stack to start grading. "As you know, you are all to be preparing for your test. I trust everyone has been studying," she said. Giving a quick glance across the room, she picked up the stack of papers, and I stopped breathing. Then she stashed them in the briefcase she brought with her, and I let out a super long sigh of relief. For the next fifty minutes, we covered vocabulary and read a portion of *To Kill A Mockingbird*, one of the coolest books ever written in my opinion. When the bell rang, I grabbed my books and jacket. I'd scored huge!

The paper was burning a hole in my backpack. I didn't dare chance taking it out during second period. Today Mr. Peterson chose to lecture. Of all days! He kept slapping page after page on the document reader. Stuff I should have found totally amazing. Instead, all I could see was the result of one man's horrible actions. Hitler's victims were on display in front of me. Helpless, tortured people. So many people.

Since my seat is in the back of the room, I could have stuck Billy's essay inside a book and read it. But since I liked this class, I was usually called on for answers. So, I sat there, listening to the lecture which lasted the entire period. My hand was nearly going in spasms by the time the class was over. I'd have writer's cramp the rest of the day from all the notes I took.

By the time third period rolled around, I was ready for orbit. Hurrying into the library, I went right into the back room and put my stuff on the desk set up for student aides. This was the period I helped out in the library. I went hunting for the head librarian, Mrs. Hernandez. When I found her, she was shelving paperbacks.

"Hi, Rachel," she smiled. "How are you today?"

"Fine," I lied. Clearing my throat, I said, "I was wondering, though, if I could ask a favor."

"Sure. What is it?

"Could I use part of the period to look over some things after I get my chore chart done today? Would that be okay with you?"

"Sure. I don't see why not," she moaned as she got up from the floor. "Have a Mrs. Bentley test coming up?" she asked with a grin.

"Yeah." I smiled.

"Knock yourself out, kiddo. If I can help, let me know."

"Thanks," I smiled at her and hurried to the circulation desk to start on my chores. Thirty minutes later everything was finished. That's when Billy Isley walked in. He headed to the periodical section and grabbed a magazine, flopping into one of the chairs in the corner.

Mrs. Hernandez walked over. "You go on. If he needs anything, I'll help him."

"Thanks. I really appreciate it, Mrs. Hernandez." In a flash, I grabbed my backpack and went into the wireless lab. No one was there, so I fished out the essay and began reading. Billy had hand-written it. From the looks of it, he had written it in big letters to cover up more space. It wasn't even close to two pages, but that was probably the best he could do. I started reading, but the more I read, the madder I got. It only took about five minutes. The thing slowing me down was the horrible grammar and punctuation.

CHAT

Bretta Deevers

Bretta Deevers was not who everyone thought she was. She was real self centerd and kind of a snob. She acted like a real hot shot, but there wasn't anything hot about her. She stole money from me once and she tole me she stole money from her folks to. I don't think what happened to her was good or nothin but people just ought to know she was kind of foney. she thought she was goin to be some hot shot artist some day but she couldn't draw that good. She never wood of made it in california. I got an uncle that lives out there and he said that theres a hole bunch of them artsie people that think there really something. There all on welfare, most of them. He works in the welfare office out there. Hes got a real good job. Anyway, Bretta was pretty to look at, but she was not real nice. I didn't know her real good, but I'm glad. She wasn't a person I'd want to hang out with, you know. Maybe thats mean to say but I believe in saying it strait. I feel reel bad for her folks. I guess they thought she was something prettie special.

Sticking the essay under another piece of paper, I peeked out the door and headed to the copier. It was on the other side of the library from Billy. Lightning quick, I copied the paper and then pulled out the notebook I found in the box. I was taking a chance having it at school, but I needed a copy of it.

When I finished copying the last of the notes between Billy and Bretta, I stuck the originals in my backpack. I made sure the copies were in my binder in case I needed to show them to Billy to make a believer out of him. I wouldn't let him near the originals. I needed to find a safe place to put those at home tonight. I put the copy of Billy's essay with my own papers. I'd give it to Mrs. Bentley and apologize for getting it mixed up with my own papers. Hopefully, she'd buy it. Even if she didn't, it would still be worth it.

Looking over at Billy, I gathered up my nerve and walked over to his table. Nobody was around so I perched on the chair nearest him. Mrs. Hernandez glanced up, and then went back to what she was doing.

Billy looked up. First, he looked surprised and then happy. He smoothed his hair back and sat up straighter. He looked like the toad he was.

"Hi," he said. "You want something'?" He looked first at my chest then at my mouth.

"Maybe," I said, leaning toward him.

"Like what?" Finally, his eyes focused on mine.

"Like maybe I'd like to eat lunch with you today." That took him by surprise.

"Lunch. Like in the lunchroom?"

"That's where it's usually served," I replied.

"Well, sure." Then he looked wary. "I ain't buyin'. You gotta buy your own."

"Did I ask you to buy my lunch?" This guy was such a jerk.

"No. But I want you to know, okay?"

"Okay. I'll see you after fourth period." I leaned closer. "And I'd like for it to be just the two of us," I whispered. I thought he was going to fall out of his seat.

I wandered back behind the circulation desk. "Is there anything else I can do to help you today, Mrs. Hernandez?"

"No, but thanks. Did you get a lot of studying done?"

"No," I said truthfully. "But I did take care of some things." That wasn't a lie. I'd studied Billy's essay carefully.

"That so." She looked at me and went to her office. By the time I walked to the back to pick up my books and jacket, the bell was ringing for fourth period. I hurried out the door. Billy left his magazine on the table for someone else to put up. Figures, I thought.

My mind raced as I hurried to art. The bell was ringing. My fourth period class was across campus in a classroom that used to be part of the old school. A wall had been knocked out for more space. Exhibits were sometimes held on one end of the classroom. Bretta's work had always been included. She loved to paint. She was gifted in sculpture and clay, too, but her first love was painting and sketching. And I didn't agree with Billy. She *had* been good. A sadness crept into my heart when I thought about Mrs. Bentley's words: "Those who loved her are left to ponder what could have been."

Class went by fast, and then the bell rang for lunch break. I hadn't had time to plan out what I was going to do! Putting my supplies away, I headed toward the lunchroom on wobbly legs. *What was the best way to get information out of Billy?* I needed to knock him off his guarded little rear if I was going to get any straight answers. I didn't really expect him to confess, but seeing his reaction to my questions would be revealing. "Please, God. Let me do this right," I whispered quietly.

I eased down the lunch line, not really caring what I picked up. I didn't want anything to eat, but he'd be suspicious if I sat down with no food. So, I chose a tuna sandwich, an apple, and a bottle of water. I paid the cashier and looked around the room. Billy was sitting at a little table in the corner. He liked corners. He was watching for me and jerked his head to motion me over. Total loser, I thought. But I needed information, and I was determined to find out as much as I could from this guy.

Squaring my shoulders, I marched to his table. He'd chosen one for two people, and I was glad. This would give us privacy. I put my tray on the table.

"What took you so long?" he asked, his mouth full of lasagna. Bits of cheese were hanging from his mouth.

"I had to walk farther." I tried to resist ending the sentence with "idiot", but the urge was pretty strong. "Art class is across campus," I pointed out. I unwrapped my sandwich and took a tiny bite. It wasn't half bad.

"So, whadaya want to talk to me about?" He winked and rubbed one of his knees against mine. My stomach knotted up.

"Bretta's murder," I said bluntly. Bits of lasagna came flying out of his mouth. Lucky for me, his tray caught most of it. He raised his hand, but it was the hurt one. He didn't waste any time in lowering it.

"What're you talking about? Some guy did her. Somebody from off somewhere. That's what the police are sayin'."

"That's because they don't know about you and Bretta," I said, staring into his face. I took a sip of water and watched his reaction.

Billy gulped and looked around him to see if anybody could hear. "I don't know what you're gettin at. Me and Bretta never dated."

"That's not true, and you know it." I took another bite of the sandwich. I was enjoying myself. I chewed carefully and swallowed, never taking my eyes off his face.

He narrowed his eyes and scooted his tray away. "What do you know?" he asked, with a sneer.

"I know about you and Bretta, Billy."

"How do you know? She swore she didn't tell nobody."

"She didn't. I found the notebook the two of you passed back and forth. It's got some hot stuff in it. It was kind of dumb to leave a paper trail, you know. It's the kind of stuff the police will love." All the color drained from his disgusting face.

"She told me she burned that," he said.

"She didn't."

"What are you going to do with it?"

"That's up to you. You tell me what happened last Saturday, and you might get it back. You don't, I give it to the police."

"You got it here at school. Like in your locker?"

"Are you stupid, Billy?" I could see the wheels turning in his head. He was trying to decide what to do. I wasn't about to admit to him that I had the thing anywhere near me.

"Okay," he said, leaning closer. "Me and Bretta, we sort of got together, you know." I nodded. That image was enough to turn my stomach. I pushed the rest of the tuna away.

"Were you mad when she dumped you?" I asked.

"I dumped her," he said, his nostrils flaring.

"Not according to the notebook. I read the note she wrote to you. And the note you wrote back. I know who dumped who."

He looked around the room and lowered his voice. "Okay. She dumped me. But I was getting ready to get rid of her anyway. I told her that in the notebook. I was tired of her. She was way too clingy. I couldn't go anywhere without her jumping me about it. 'Course, she wasn't with me all the time. I got me plenty of chicks. She just didn't know about it," he bragged. "She wasn't nothin' but a tease."

"You were mad when she broke it off?"

"Yeah, I was mad. No chick's ever cut it off with me. I was mad enough to kill her, the ..." He broke off the rest of the sentence, realizing what he'd said.

"So did you?" I leaned forward, trying to intimidate him.

"Did I what?" he asked nervously.

"Did you kill Bretta? You just said you were mad enough to. Did you?"

Billy looked down. "I was mad, but I didn't kill her. There's plenty of other girls out there that want to be with me, you know."

"How'd you hurt your hand?" I asked.

He flinched. "None of your business."

I stared at him with one eyebrow cocked. "Okay, if that's the way you want it," I said, rising.

"I sliced it while I was fishin'. My knife slipped while I was cutting' the line. You satisfied, snoop?"

"Where's your knife now?"

"It fell over the side of the boat," he growled.

"It's a shame to lose a good knife. Real convenient, too."

"You gonna give me back my notebook?" he growled.

I looked at him and shrugged, gathering up my stuff. "Haven't decided." I walked away and put my tray on the stand by the exit. I felt his hot gaze blazing on my back. Not for a million dollars would I chance looking at him.

Part of me felt really pumped, like I'd finally taken a step toward getting Bretta's killer. But a tiny voice inside kept telling me to be careful. I shoved the dread clear outside. I wanted to do this. I was going to do this.

I hurried to find Mrs. Bentley. Fifth period was her planning period, and I was sure she'd start grading our papers. I needed to get Billy's essay to her. If I waited until tomorrow, she'd be suspicious. I saw her going to the teacher's lounge so I walked faster. I caught her as she placed her hand on the door. She gave me a puzzled look and cocked her head.

"Is there something I can do for you, Rachel?" she asked curtly.

"I apologize, Mrs. Bentley. I didn't turn in all the papers this morning. Billy's got mixed up with some of my own papers. Here," I said, shoving the paper in her direction. "I knew you'd want it before you started grading. I'm really sorry." When I looked at her face, her eyes narrowed. Pure loathing came from them and I took a half step backward. I figured she wouldn't be happy about my having the paper, but I wasn't prepared for the look of disgust I was getting.

"You just found the paper?" she demanded.

"No," I replied. "I found it third period." That was partially true. I hadn't had time to look at it until then.

"I see," she said, looking carefully at the paper. She cocked her head to the left as if deciding how to best handle this. "I saw the two of you eating together. I didn't realize you were friends. Are you friendly enough that you might write an essay for him, Rachel?

"I was so shocked all I could do was stand there with my mouth open. "No," I nearly shouted. "I can't stand Billy Isley!" Then, realizing I'd probably made a fool out of myself, I stepped back.

"I'll find the folder containing first period assignments and add it. In the future, I'm sure you'll be more careful."

"I will. I'm sorry, Mrs. Bentley," I said, backing down the corridor. "It won't happen again. I promise." I hurried to my fifth period class. Mr. Hunter frowned on tardiness. I had to practically run to make it to his room on time. Lucky for me my seat is at the front of the room.

I took out my textbook, but my mind wasn't on civics. It was on Billy Isley and the essay he wrote. Once Bentley saw it, I was pretty sure she'd get that I hadn't written it. Still, it surprised me that she'd accuse me of doing that.

Billy was a jerk. Plus, he had a strong motive for wanting Bretta dead. She embarrassed him by dumping him. She bashed his ego. He got mad fast. I just witnessed that. He also admitted to owning a knife. But did he really have it in him to kill somebody? Something Billy said at lunch nagged at me. I didn't have all the answers, but I was going to find them.

NINE

By the end of Wednesday, I felt wiped out. Thankfully, I didn't have another class with Billy. I passed him in the hall one time, and I could feel how mad he was from ten feet away. His glare told me he wanted the notebook back, and he wanted it now. I could always give it back, but if Billy really had killed Bretta, he'd get rid of it. Then an important piece of evidence would be gone. No, I'd hang on to it until I figured things out.

Mr. Keely didn't assign homework so I could spend my time on Bentley's study guide tonight. I needed to go over my notes from Mr. Peterson, but I could do that over the weekend. His tests were always on Tuesdays.

When I walked out of math, Mrs. Doyle was standing in the hall, talking to some of the students. She looked up and smiled at me, then she followed me to my locker.

"Hi, Rachel. How are you?" she asked.

People were asking me that a lot lately. "I'm okay," I said. I turned around to look at her. "Actually, I do have a problem I'd like to discuss with you."

Her face lit up. "Sure. How about now?"

"I can't right now. I'm going over to Pam Nichol's house to study for a test. Could we talk tomorrow or Friday?"

"That would be great. When would be a good time?" she asked.

"I might be able to leave after I finish with Mrs. Bentley's test first period— if it doesn't last the whole period," I offered.

"That would be fine. I'll speak with her this afternoon and see if she has any objections. We have a faculty meeting in the library." I would be relieved to talk to her about the dad dilemma. Maybe she could talk to Mom and tell her what a mistake this was going to be.

A few minutes later, I stood outside the front door looking for Pam. I was surprised when I spotted Mom in the pick-up lane. I walked toward the car.

"Didn't you get my message?" I asked. I knew she could sense the irritation in my voice.

"I did. I wanted to make sure you were okay." Another person checking to see if I was okay.

"I'm fine, Mom. This morning upset me. You could have talked to me about it, you know. I'm not a little kid anymore. I thought you trusted my opinion. Guess I was wrong."

"I do trust you. I also know you feel betrayed by your father." A horn sounded from behind her. We were holding up the line.

"I have to go, Mom. I'll call you later if I need a ride home. Pam's mother will probably bring me. It'll be around 9:00. Okay?"

She nodded, glancing over her shoulder. "Hand me the stuff you won't need, and I'll take it home for you. Then you won't have as much to carry.

"Okay," I said, plopping my heavy backpack on the curb. "I'll take out my notes." The horn blared again. I pulled out my three-ring binder holding the copies of Billy's notebook and essay, and Mrs. Bentley's handout. I shoved the rest of the stuff back in and threw it into the passenger seat. "Thanks," I mumbled, stepping back from the car.

"I love you, Rachel."

"I know," I said, eyeing the car in the rear. They were really getting steamed. "I love you, too." Mom glanced in her rearview mirror and put the car into gear to pull through the line. Feeling a tap on my shoulder, I turned around, half expecting to find Billy Isley in my face. I was glad to see Pam instead.

"Hi. Still want to tackle Bentley's handout?" she asked with a smile. She looked in the direction of Mom's car.

"You bet. I told Mom I'd be home by nine. I wasn't sure how long it would take us."

"That's perfect. We like to loosen up before we start studying. We'll have a snack and get organized and start studying about 5:00. Sound okay?"

"Sounds great. This day's been really long."

"Yeah. For me, too. I wish we didn't have this test to study for, but I guess there's no getting out of it."

"Guess not. But it'll help having a group to study with," I said.

"It really does. A bunch of us started this back in January, and it's worked out great. I think you're gonna like it. Plus, my mom makes really good pizzas."

I smiled and realized I was starving. Breakfast was in the trash, and I had eaten only a few bites of tuna at lunch.

"There's Mom," Pam said, pointing to a blue minivan pulling up in line. "You ready?" I nodded and climbed in. I settled back on the seat and began to relax. Then, glancing out the window, I noticed Billy standing a few feet from where Pam and I had been. An uneasy feeling swelled inside me. Pam started talking about the other girls in the group, and I focused on listening to her. By the time we arrived at Pam's house, I was laughing and having a good time. *This is nice.*

We walked into the house, and Pam told us to pile our stuff on her bed. I followed her into the kitchen and was immediately handed a big bowl and some packets of popcorn.

"You don't mind being the popcorn girl, do ya?" she grinned.

"Not a bit," I said, carrying them over to the microwave. The doorbell sounded, and Pam hurried to let in four more girls from our class. The next thirty minutes were spent munching and talking.

From there, the study session got better. I worried the girls might think I was as snobby as Bretta had been. I didn't want that. I wanted friends—more than one.

When the smell of homemade pizzas floated through the house, all six of us clambered into the kitchen. I closed my eyes for a second and took a deep breath. Katelyn Hawley nudged me.

"You taking a nap?" she asked. "'Cause if you are, I get your pizza."

"Forget it," I grinned. "Nobody would give up a piece of that," I said, pointing to the first one being pulled out of the oven. The mozzarella was bubbling, and the crust was golden.

The next three hours passed fast. We ate, we visited, we laughed —and then we got down to serious studying. There were six of us, and the group had been doing this since January, so they were organized. Everyone went to a different place in the den and started going over Bentley's handout. Pam set the timer for thirty minutes. They called this the self-study time.

I made a list of all the important information. Mom was always teasing me about my lists. Listing helped me think and remember important things. That was what I did when I needed to remember something. Next to my journal, listing was my favorite way to organize myself.

When the buzzer went off, everybody picked a partner. This time, each person took fifteen minutes to quiz the other one. The next fifteen minutes we switched. When the next buzzer went off, we changed partners. By the time we finished, we all had at least three partners, and everyone had asked questions over everything on the study guide. The only thing left to do after that was print out a practice test on the computer. All we had to do was find a test program on Google, put in Bentley's information, punch trial test, and wait for the printer to spit out the tests. These girls knew what they were doing. This group was great. Now, I was ready for Bentley and her test.

"What's that?" Jerzie Peterson asked, springing up from the floor.

Her partner, Leslie Michaels sniffed the air. "Ohhh. I know that smell." She headed to the kitchen with the rest of us right behind her.

"Cinnamon rolls," gasped Leslie. "Oh, yum! Can we try one, Mrs. Nichols?"

"I'll be crushed if you don't eat at least three," Pam's mom replied.

"My mom raised me to never hurt anybody's feelings," Lisa Morgan said with a grin.

"Good, then dig in." She handed the spatula to me. Pam grabbed the paper plates, and I dished up the hot buns. They were dripping with creamy, white icing. Pam's mom carried the milk jug over.

Leslie moaned. "My mom's aren't nearly this good, but don't any of you tell her I said that."

"You're lucky, Pam," Katelyn said. "My mom can't boil water. We have take-out everything."

Pam looked proud. I felt guilty. Mom had gone to a lot of trouble fixing my breakfast this morning. She probably hadn't slept much, and I hadn't even thanked her. Instead, I blew up over the whole Dad thing. But what she'd done was wrong, wasn't it? I should be part of the decision-making. I listened to the chatter around me.

"So next week, we'll meet at my house," Lisa was saying. "We'll probably only have chips and dip," she said apologetically.

"If we ate like this every week, we'd look like whales," Jerzie said. "Y'all know how my mom cooks. If it can't be micro-waved, forget it." She grinned. "But that's okay." We all nodded. I needed to apologize to Mom when I got home. Maybe we could talk for a while. I looked at the clock. It was already 8:45.

"I've got to go," I said to Pam. "I told Mom I'd be home by nine, and I don't want her to worry." I took my fork and glass to the sink. We all started putting our coats on.

Pam's mom frowned. "We have a little problem." Everyone stopped and looked at Mrs. Nichols. She was standing in the entryway wiping her hands on a kitchen towel. She looked worried and embarrassed.

"What is it?" Pam asked.

"I'm afraid I wasn't thinking very well about how to get everyone home. We've been so used to having five girls in the group," she shrugged.

"The van holds seven, Mom, plus the driver." She gave her mom one of those looks that said she'd been standing over the stove too long, and her brain had melted.

"But your dad came and got the van after I got all of you here. It's in the shop," Mrs. Nichols explained. "He left the car."

"The van is in the shop?" Pam repeated. "Oh! And the car will only hold four plus you," Pam said. "Well, I can stay behind and clean up. No," she said, ticking the names of her friends on her fingers. That still won't help. We have a problem." Her mom rolled her eyes.

"There's not a problem," I said. "I only live five minutes away. You have to go in the other direction anyway to take everybody else home. I'll be there in no time if I jog. The rain's stopped, and I like to run. Besides, after all this food, I need the exercise," I grinned.

"I don't know," Mrs. Nichols said, worry showing on her face.

"Not a good idea," Pam said. "Not a good idea …"

I took a deep breath. "I'll be fine. I'll even call the second I get in the door."

"Have you got your cell phone with you?" asked Pam. "Your mom could run over and pick you up."

I patted my pocket. "I've got it, but Mom's really tired. And besides, I'm telling you, I'll be home before I could even get off the phone with her." I smiled. "Stop worrying. This is not a problem."

Jerzie was looking worried. She glanced at the clock. "I really have to go pretty soon. My mom is a huge worrier. She's used to me being home by now."

"Me, too," Leslie chimed.

"Settled," I said. "I promise I'll call Pam the second I get home, Mrs. Nichols, and thanks for including me tonight." Before anybody could argue, I raced out the door— and straight into the biggest fog I've ever seen. The streetlights were on, but it didn't really help. It was like trying to see through thick soup.

I went a block when I realized my jacket wasn't going to help much. It kept the rain out, but the damp cold was seeping right through the rubber material. I shivered and picked up my pace.

I heard a vehicle coming and moved off the street. It was safer to walk in the wet grass than to worry about traffic. My shoes were soaked almost immediately, and I was getting really cold. Then I realized the vehicle I heard was slowing down. The happiness I felt a few minutes ago was shoved out by fear. The sound of the engine was coming closer. I moved farther onto the grass to give whoever was behind me plenty of room. The vehicle slowed even more. Maybe the driver was waiting to pull into one of the driveways.

Two blocks from home, I glanced over my shoulder and saw dim headlights glowing from the other side of the street. Whoever was behind me had pulled to the other side of the street and faced the wrong direction. What was with that?

The fog was so thick I could barely see the vehicle to make out the color or see the outline. Seeing inside was impossible. The van seemed longer than most family vans. I remembered the conversation between Aunt Jane and Mom. Someone saw a van the day Bretta died. I froze.

Then I heard a door slide open.

That was all it took for my mind to snap into gear. I leaped off the slippery grass and ran down the street. I heard another sound behind me. But it wasn't footsteps. It was a different engine sound. I turned, stepped out into the street, and waved to the car coming up behind me. I heard a door sliding shut, and then the van engine revved up, reversed, and took off down a side street. I was so relieved I nearly passed out, The car I waved down pulled to the side of the road.

It was Leslie's head that poked out of the window. "Are you okay? Who was that?" she asked.

"I don't know," I admitted. My entire body was shaking, and Mrs.

Nichols was out of the car in a shot.

"You don't know who was in that van?" She asked. She put both arms around me and patted my back. "Are you okay?" She looked at my face. I nodded and tried to give her a reassuring smile. From the look on her face, I must not have convinced her.

"What are y'all doing here?" I asked.

"Mrs. Nichols got worried and decided to follow you home," Katelyn said from the back seat. "We called our moms to let 'em know we'd be late. Rachel, come on. You can sit on my lap. You're not walking anymore." I knew I should probably be brave and say no, but the truth was, I was scared so bad my knees shook. So, climbing into the car, I sat on Katelyn's legs for the next block. It took all of two minutes to get me home.

"I'm waiting right here until you get in the house. And you tell your mom what happened. Do you want me to come and talk to her?"

"No, I'll tell her. Thanks, everybody." I knew my voice was shaking, but they all seemed okay with that.

"See you tomorrow, Rachel," they called. I waved to them and dug out my house key. Closing the door behind me, I leaned against it and sighed. "Thank you, God," I prayed. Aunt Jane had always sworn I had a sixth sense. Tonight, I believed her. I knew the minute that van pulled over that something really dangerous was driving it.

Pulling off my wet gear, I hung my jacket on the hall tree. The house was quiet. The fire was crackling, and I expected to find Mom asleep on the couch. I was ready to tell her what had happened. She needed to know. I'd even tell her how I felt about Dad coming home.

Quietly, I put all my stuff on the floor and headed toward the kitchen, flipping the light switch as I went. No light. I nearly tripped over Edna. She was curled on top of a house shoe, her normal hangout during fog. Great, I thought. The light bulb burned out. I headed toward the storage closet where we keep the bulbs. As I was passing her room, I peeked in to check on Aunt Jane.

Her room was dark. I flipped on her switch. No light. Two lights and neither of them working? A little too weird. Pulling the door shut, I turned around and headed toward the stairs. That's when I checked the fridge door – our note exchange place – and saw the note tacked to the refrigerator with one of my old homemade magnets. Pulling it off the door, I went to the sink, flipping the switch that should have lit up the overhead light. It didn't. Walking back to the fridge, I opened the door. No reassuring little light popped on. An uneasy feeling started in the pit of my stomach and worked its way into my throat. I slid open the junk drawer beside the fridge and felt around for the metal flashlight Mom kept there, whispering a little prayer that it was still there. My hand fumbled around and finally touched the old-fashioned metal cylinder. One flip and the light glowed. I sent up a thank you prayer and then read the note.

Rachel, Had to leave. Emergency at the shop.

Will be home as soon as possible. Love Mom.

I read it again. There wasn't a time jotted anywhere on it, so I didn't know how long they'd been gone. Had the electricity been off when they left? Mom would have mentioned that in the note. And what had happened at the shop? Reaching for the phone on the wall, I laid the message on the table and heard Edna purring. She followed me into the kitchen. As I reached down to pick her up, I realized no dial tone was coming from the receiver.

I heard another noise. This one was not familiar. I switched off the flashlight and stood still, listening.

Silently, I moved toward the back door, clutching Edna. Her ears were pricked and twitching. She heard it, too, and started to squirm. She wanted down. As soon as I set her on the floor, she rocketed into the laundry room. I watched her go, and I started toward the back door to check out the noise. Under my feet, something crunched. I flicked the flashlight on again and saw pieces of glass on the floor. Pointing my flashlight beam toward the door, I swallowed hard. One pane of glass was shattered. Had Mom or Aunt Jane broken it accidentally? No. They wouldn't leave glass on the floor, no matter what had happened in the shop. They would have worried about Edna getting cut.

No lights. No phone. Broken glass. Break in.

That person could still be in the house! I looked around for something to grab. My eyes fell on Mom's skillet. I put the flimsy flashlight on the counter and picked up the heavy pan. I took a step away from the stove and caught a movement from outside. I stepped into the shadows of the kitchen and watched as a figure came up to the back door. If I moved now, he would hear me. I watched as a hand reached through the glass. The knob turned. I held my breath. I could see Mom's cell phone on the table. I reached for mine. It wasn't there. Had it fallen out while I was running? Silently, I prayed. If I made a dash for Mom's phone then ran up the stairs, would I have time to get to my room and lock the door before the person grabbed me? Probably not.

I took a deep breath and shut my eyes for just a second. The door creaked open. I held the skillet so hard my hands hurt. The figure stopped and listened. He seemed to be looking around the kitchen. The light from the streetlight cast a ghost of a glow in the room. Quickly, I stepped out of the shadows and raised my weapon. With as much strength as I could manage, I swung it. The cast iron skillet made contact with the intruder's head. A sickening *thud* sounded, and the body fell to the floor.

With shaking hands, I reached for the phone and moved as far away from the body as I could without losing sight of it. I ended up pressed up against the refrigerator. After two tries I punched in the emergency numbers. My eyes looked at the figure who was lying face down on the floor. I was waiting for the slightest movement. I dropped the skillet beside the still form.

"Hello. What is your emergency?" The voice from the other end of the connection startled me, and I jumped.

"Help me," I said.

"What is the nature of your emergency?"

"I hit him," I knew I wasn't making any sense. "I hit— someone with my mom's skillet. I think he may be dead. I don't hear him breathing." My voice sounded funny, like I was trying to scream the words.

"An officer is on his way. I'll send for an ambulance. Stay on the line, please." I was about to tell her that would be no problem when I noticed the body on the floor was moving his foot. His arm was moving, too. He was trying to turn over.

"Miss, did you hear me?" The voice on the other end asked.

"He's moving," I whispered.

"Go into another room, but don't hang up," the woman said urgently. "Can you go into a room and lock the door? Do so immediately."

I tried to tell my feet to move. I wanted my body to run up the stairs, but I couldn't move. The only person who seemed to be able to do that was the person on the floor. My mouth went dry. I could hear the woman's voice. It sounded like it was far away. The body turned over. I recognized the face. I stared, and then I dropped the phone.

The man lying on the floor with blood all over his face—was my dad.

TEN

I stared at my father. Blood poured from the wound. I was barely aware of a woman's voice floating up from the floor. I grabbed the phone.

"It's my dad," I cried. "I've hit my dad. He's bleeding. Help!"

"The police and ambulance should be there any minute," the woman said. "Can your father speak?"

"Dad," I said, kneeling beside him. "Dad, are you okay?" I tried to put my hand under his elbow to help him up, but I slipped in something wet. The phone went skidding across the floor. Landing on the floor beside him, I realized I was sitting in the blood from his head wound.

I heard the scream of an ambulance and could see flashing blue lights out the window. I started to get up, and slipped again. Dad had collapsed back onto the floor. My heart pounded. Was he dead? What if I killed him? I knew I hit him hard. Crawling over to the door, I swung it open.

"We're back here," I screamed. Holding to the counter top, I stood on shaky legs. I tried the lights again, but nothing happened. A policeman appeared with a gun in his hand. A few steps away, were the EMT crew. I pointed to Dad.

"What happened?" asked the officer, his feet crunching in the glass.

"I thought he was a robber. I hit him with my mom's skillet," I confessed, lip trembling. "I think I really hurt him. He tried to get up, but he couldn't. And there's a lot of blood," I said, pointing to the growing puddle on the floor.

"Bud," the officer hollered out the door. "You guys better get in here. We've got a severe head wound."

In moments, the emergency team was crouching around Dad, placing oxygen on his face and taking his vitals. The beams from the policeman's flashlight, plus those of the ambulance workers, were shining on Dad. He started to moan and move around. I watched, terrified that his movements would stop. Then I heard the front door open and close. More footsteps were pounding through the house.

"What in the world is going on?" demanded Mom. I hurried to her side. She was fumbling for the light switch.

"It doesn't work," I said, going to her. "The lights were off when I got home."

"None of them work?" Aunt Jane asked. "What happened to them?"

"I don't know. When I got home, the whole house was dark. I found the flashlight and read your note, and then …"

But Mom had tuned me out. She was staring at Dad.

"Oh, my dear God," she cried, hurrying to his side. "Steve, are you all right?" Aunt Jane moved beside me and put her arm around my shoulders.

"Mom," I said. She didn't answer. She was watching Dad's face. In the light from all the flashlights, he looked bad. Very bad.

I turned to Aunt Jane. "I didn't mean to hurt Dad," I said, tears slipping down my cheek. "I thought he was a burglar or something. I got spooked when I got home, and no one was here. And then the lights were off and the glass was broken."

"This glass?" the officer asked. Another man, in regular clothes was with him. Both were examining the door and the shattered mess.

"Yeah," I answered. "I found it when I came in the kitchen. Then

I saw someone reach in and turn the door handle. I guess I panicked. I was so sure it was a burglar." I said again. "I hit him with Mom's frying pan."

"You did the same thing anyone would have done," Aunt Jane soothed. "You didn't know it was your father." She gave my shoulder another squeeze and led me into the den. "Let's wait in here until they get finished," she urged.

"Is everything okay at the shop?" I asked, glancing back at Dad. Mom was trying to hover over him, and the emergency crew was having a hard time working around her.

Aunt Jane shoved me gently onto the couch and sat close to me, patting my hand.

"Well, that's a strange thing," she said, shaking her head. "We received a phone call about an hour ago saying the shop had been broken into. I didn't think to ask who was making the call. We assumed it was one of the neighbors. Anyway, your mom scribbled a quick note to you, and we zoomed out of here. But, when we got there, everything looked fine. We waited outside for a while to see if the police were going to show up. Then we went and called them at Barney's. You know, the guy that has the all-night diner across the street. They showed up, and we all went in, but nothing was missing that we could see. The door hadn't been broken into either." She looked toward the kitchen. "I'm beginning to think someone wanted us out of the house," she said. "It looks like this is the place they wanted to rob, not the shop." She squeezed my shoulders.

I shivered and wondered how long the burglar had been gone. Had the person been there when I came home? Was it Dad Edna and I heard outside or someone else? I looked around. Aunt Jane noticed and looked around, too.

"I don't see anything missing," she said. "Maybe you scared them off." She smiled, and then hugged me to her. "It scares me senseless to think you might have been hurt. She settled herself more comfortably on the couch and motioned for me to light one of Mom's candles on the coffee table. I went around the room lighting as many as I could find. Each one made the room lighter. It helped to have something to do. By the time I finished, the room wasn't dark. I kept glancing toward the kitchen. I heard a loud moan.

"I'm fine," I heard a muffled voice say. I rushed into the kitchen in time to see Dad sitting up. He was trying to remove the oxygen mask they placed over his face.

"Dad, I'm so sorry. I didn't know it was you," I explained through tears.

"It's my fault. I didn't know you were home. You did the right thing. You were protecting yourself."

"But when did you get here?" Mom asked, her hand on his arm. When he looked down at it, she moved it to her side.

"About thirty minutes ago."

"I only texted this morning," she said. "How did you get here so fast?"

He cleared his throat and put his hand to his head. Wincing, he said, "I asked a pilot friend of mine to fly me in as soon as he could." He glared at the ambulance worker who was pressing on his cut.

"Sorry," the man muttered. "But we've got to get the bleeding stopped." He kept right on pressing.

"I got here as soon as I could and then hired a taxi to get me to the house. When I stepped out of the taxi, I saw someone running out the back door. I ran after him, but in this fog, I lost whoever it was. I walked around the block, thinking I might spot a car or something, but I didn't see anything. I thought I heard some tires screeching, but I couldn't see where it was," he said, frustration evident in his voice. "I guess whoever it was thought no one was home. There was no car in the drive. They probably watched the house for a while to monitor any movement." Dad shrugged.

Mom looked at Aunt Jane, who had come to stand beside me. They exchanged a meaningful glance. "I think whoever broke in tonight knew we wouldn't be home." She told him about the false alarm at the shop.

He nodded. "Yeah, I'm sure you're right. Someone set this up, but they didn't plan on me coming in when I did." I wondered how they knew I wouldn't be home. There was no guarantee I would go with Mom and Aunt Jane to the shop.

"Anyway," he continued, "when I got back to the house, I thought I could see the beam of a flashlight. I was convinced there must have been two intruders. Now, I realize what I saw was you, and," he said, looking at me, "I guess you thought I was the bad guy." He smiled a weak smile. "It's alright, Kitten."

I flinched. He hadn't called me that in six years. I turned away from him and watched as the police officer went outside.

"What time did you get home?" Mom asked, turning to me.

"A little after 9:00." Now wasn't the time to tell her about the van. I could tell from the look on her face she already had all the shocks she needed for a while.

The ambulance workers were finishing up the bandaging on Dad's head. He insisted on moving to the kitchen table but slipped on the bloody puddle beneath him. I could hear the policeman outside talking. Then a crackling noise sounded, and I heard a voice from the other end of his radio, but I couldn't make out what it was saying. He stepped back inside.

"It looks like your electrical box has been ripped off the back of the house," he announced.

"What?" Mom said, alarm in her voice. "Who would do that? Why would anyone want to break in here in the first place? We don't own anything worth stealing."

"Can you give me a description, Mr. Reynolds?" asked the policeman, turning to Dad. He towered over all of us.

Dad shook his head. "No. The fog was too thick. And whoever broke in was fast. If I'd been here a few minutes earlier, I could have caught him." His eyes moved to the arch leading into the den. Aunt Jane stood under it, looking at her brother. She looked like someone in a trance. Her head was tilted and she watched Dad's every move. I caught something in Dad's face when he looked at his sister. Even in the dark, it looked a lot like guilt.

Then the moment was over and we all took turns answering questions. Mom and Aunt Jane couldn't offer much. They left around 7:30 to go to the shop. The lights had been working. No, they hadn't noticed any suspicious cars.

I glanced at the clock on the mantel. We were all sitting in front of the fire, trying to remember everything about the evening. It was almost eleven. The EMT's were long gone, and we were yawning. The policeman, who had introduced himself as Officer Selie, closed his notebook and stood up. The guy with him stared a lot. The kind of stare that made butterflies do somersaults in my stomach.

Something about his stare prompted me to tell him about the van. The other stuff I'd keep to myself for now. After all, I had no proof of who the person was that broke in.

"There is one thing," I said. Officer Selie stopped as he was about to tuck his notepad into his pocket. He turned to me but not with a lot of interest. He probably had kids of his own. I saw the same look on Mom's face when she was tired and I was babbling about something stupid. But this time, the something I needed to tell them was important.

I cleared my throat. At first, my words rushed out. I was afraid I would lose my nerve if I didn't tell them fast. Looking at the confused faces, I realized I was stumbling over words and not making much sense. Taking a deep breath, I started again. "I was walking home from a study group tonight …"

"You walked home!" Mom said, sitting straight up in her chair. "Why on earth did you do that? Oh no," she said, her head in her hands. "You probably did try to call, didn't you? And I left my phone on the kitchen table. That's my fault," she said, misery written all over her face. "I left in such a hurry, I forgot to take it with me. But that's not an excuse. I should have called you at Pam's house instead of just leaving a note. Rachel, I don't want you going anywhere alone."

"Mom, relax," I said, holding up my hands. "No, I didn't try to call. It was only a few blocks," I said, explaining everything to her. I also told the cop that my phone had probably fallen out of my pocket when I was running.

"Why were you running?" Mom asked. She didn't miss much.

"Everything is okay. You're right," I hurried to say. "It was a really bad idea. I'm sorry." Oh, great. She was already stressing out, and I hadn't even told her about the van yet. Another deep breath.

"Anyway, it was really foggy, and I was jogging. I heard an engine coming, so I stepped onto the grass. It slowed and stopped but it swung over to the other side of the street. When Mrs. Nichols came along in her car, it took off." I'd been talking in the general direction of the floor. I sneaked a glance at Mom. Her white face said it all. I deliberately didn't mention the danger I felt. Maybe that had been just a case of nerves anyway. It wouldn't help to worry her more.

Both policemen wore serious frowns. "Can you describe it," one of them asked.

"No. It was too foggy, like Dad said. It looked like a dark color, and I think it was really long, like a van. I heard the engine coming from behind me. I tried to see who was inside, but with the fog and dark," I shrugged. "Sorry," I said in a lame voice.

"It's okay." Both men nodded, but only Officer Selie made notes. "We've had several break-ins in this neighborhood, though. This isn't the first. They may all be tied together."

"Did anyone else see a van prior to the robbery?" asked Dad.

"No," Selie answered. "Your daughter is the first. Maybe this is the break we've been looking for. We'll have the officers on duty watching for any suspicious vehicles, particularly a van."

Pure relief. Normally, I would not be glad to hear about neighborhood robberies, but if there were others, that meant our house hadn't been singled out. I hadn't been singled out. I was worrying for nothing. It was like the officer said, a random break-in.

So— I chose not to mention Billy Isley. If I did, I'd have to explain about the notebook. I'd have to turn it over to them. And for some reason, that seemed like I was letting Bretta down. I wanted to do this myself. It was important to wait until I had more evidence of Billy's guilt before I approached the police.

"We'll call someone about your electricity," the plainclothes man said.

"Thanks," Mom said. She walked him to the door, then returned to the kitchen.

Aunt Jane and I started cleaning up. Dad wanted to help, telling us he was okay. He swept up the glass on the floor, stopping every once in a while to check something on the door.

"I'll call Homer tomorrow," he announced. "He can put a new glass in for us." The room grew quiet.

"Homer died last year," Aunt Jane said. It was the first words she'd uttered since giving her small contribution to the night's events. Her words hung in the air, heavy and cold.

"Oh," Dad said.

Awkward moment. I excused myself from the room. "I think I'll go to bed," I said.

"Okay," Mom said, coming over to hug me. She held me close. "We'll talk tomorrow," she whispered. "I know this is sudden. For me, too."

Nodding, I grabbed up a candle and hurried to my room, relieved to be away from all the drama downstairs. In a weird way, the break-in had bonded us all. Now, things were off again. I couldn't wait to get to my own room, but the minute I topped the stairs I knew something was wrong. My bedroom door was wide open. I *never* leave my bedroom door open. Mom never leaves my bedroom door open. Too many times, I've found chewed and shredded clothes Edna has taken her frustration out on.

I bolted down the stairs. Six eyes looked startled when I came to a skidding halt at the base of the stairs. Even Edna, strolling across the floor, looked surprised. Blushing, I apologized. "Sorry. Forgot my notes down here." I grabbed the three-ring binder and tried really hard to slow my steps going back up the stairs. What I really wanted to do was take them two at a time.

Alone in my room, I raised my candle and sucked in my breath. Someone had been in here. My backpack lay on the bed, and everything had been dumped out. Papers were scattered everywhere.

I looked at the binder in my hand. Then I looked at the papers on my bed. Putting the candle on my nightstand, I unzipped the binder. There was Bentley's handout. Under that, tucked in a pocket and folded was the copy of Billy's essay as well as the photocopy of his and Bretta's notes.

I stared hard at the backpack on the bed. Then I tried to remember what happened after school. Mom pulling up. Horn honking. Me grabbing papers.

I made myself sift through the papers in front of me. But I knew I had accidentally left the original notebook in my backpack.

And now, the original notebook was gone.

Pacing, I bit one thumbnail and tried to calm down. I still had the copy, but I didn't think it would work as evidence. I needed the original. But I didn't have it. Either Billy had set this whole thing up and broken in or he'd had someone else do it for him. I knew he was a jerk, but breaking and entering, destruction of property? Did he have the sense to plan this?

I fell onto the bed, shoving the mess of papers to the side. Picking up the copies of the notebook, I decided to put them with Bretta's shoes in the closet. Then I did the thing that always made me feel better. Journal.

I bent over, grabbed my dictionary, and went across the floor to my desk. Pulling the drawer open, I yanked the journal out and hurried back to the bed. I opened my journal, marked it at the next blank page and then found the G section in the dictionary. I'd search for the right word to use tonight, but first, I needed a little one-on-one time with God. Instead of getting better, things were getting worse. I needed to ask Him to guide my head so I'd know what to do.

Please God. I'm not good at pretty praying. We've already figured that out. But I'm worried, and now I've really messed up. Show me what to do.

I opened my eyes and felt like at least part of the weight lifted off my shoulders. No. There was no instant answer, but Mom always told me that sharing the problem lightened the load. Now I get what she meant. I shared the load with God and even though there was no magical fix to all this, it was great to know he had my back.

I looked at my journal. Now I could put my thoughts on paper, but first I wanted to write down all the questions that were knocking around in my head.

Thursday a.m. 12:15

Who knew I was going to Pam's house this afternoon to study?

Someone followed me in a big vehicle from Pam's house. Who?

Was it Billy? Why would he do that if he already had the notebook?

(To scare me. Maybe it was a warning to leave him alone.) Maybe somebody was waiting for him in the van)?

When had Dad really gotten here? Had he heard noises and gone to check them out, or was he just saying that?

Dad said he got here after Mom and Aunt Jane had left. Convenient? No, now I'm thinking crazy. Had to be a coincidence. My own father can't be a suspect.

Nobody but Billy would gain anything from breaking into the house. Right???

But if Billy was busy breaking in, who was driving the van? Had I just imagined feeling like I was in danger?

I looked at the G page open beside me. It had fallen open to page 542. Glancing at the entries, I saw one that made my eyes widen.

CHAT

Gambit: **any maneuver by which one seeks to gain an advantage.**

My entry was short.

Billy Isley's **gambit** *worked. He gained the advantage tonight.*

ELEVEN

*T*hursday morning came too soon. After sleeping a couple of hours, I woke up and decided I might as well get ready. I pulled myself out of bed, listening for the morning sounds, but the house was quiet. I stretched and remembered last night.

Shaking my head, I tried to clear my brain, but it didn't work. There were so many things I didn't understand, but I was pretty sure Billy was responsible for getting Mom and Aunt Jane out of the house last night. He was close by when Pam and I talked about the study group. He must have decided right then to break into our house and get his notebook. Nothing else was missing. Dad believed he scared the burglar off before he had a chance to take anything. Not true.

The police would be furious at me now if I went to them and told them I had the notebook and then let it get stolen. Instead of getting myself out of trouble, all I was doing was making it worse.

I started down the stairs—a lot slower than last night. When I was almost to the bottom, I smelled pancakes. It was only six thirty, and there weren't any lights. Evidently, the electricity was still off. That would explain why it was so cold in the house. The heater hadn't been on all night, and that left only the fireplace for heat. Still, Mom was at the stove, flipping flapjacks. Thank goodness for gas stoves.

"I'm sorry about last night," she began, as I entered the kitchen.

"I mean, about the way you had to find out your dad was here." She raised both hands. I knew she had to be tired. The dark circles under her eyes told me she hadn't slept, *again*. But here she was, cooking breakfast for me *again*. I promised not to make this morning a repeat of yesterday.

"It's okay, Mom. I wasn't happy about you asking him to come home because of my stupid nightmare. I think you should have included me in the decision, but he's here now. And it's not a completely bad thing." I stopped and started again. "Well, me hitting him with the skillet was, but you know what I mean. In a way, it's good he was here last night, you know." Relief spread across her face.

"He never responded." she sighed, turning another pancake. "I was so angry all day, thinking he really *didn't* care about us anymore. Then when I saw him here, lying on the floor like that ..." She stopped and took a deep breath. "Last night, after you went to bed, we talked for a long time. He has vacation time built up. He left San Diego as soon as he could."

I looked at the floor. Maybe a little part of him did still care. He called me Kitten last night. Then I remembered how I hit him. "Where did he stay last night?" I asked.

"He stayed in the guest room. I was uneasy about him traveling with his injury. How do you feel about him staying here for a while?"

I nodded, glad she was finally including me in *some* decision. "You don't think he's, like, permanently hurt from last night, do you?" I asked, frowning.

"No. I don't. He's always had a thick head." She smiled and brought a plate of pancakes to me. "He left half an hour ago. He didn't sleep much last night. Neither did I," she said with a yawn. "We had a lot to talk about."

"What took Dad so long to come home?"

She shrugged. "I guess it took you being in danger to get his attention."

"But, I'm not in danger, Mom. A silly nightmare doesn't mean

I'm in danger." I took a bite of the pancakes. They were great. She made them with blueberries— my favorite.

She put the spatula down and came and sat in the chair nearest mine. "The story about Bretta was picked up by the Associated Press, Rachel. That means it's appeared in newspapers all over the country. It's all over the web. Your father read about it online in California before I ever contacted him about your nightmare. He told me last night he requested vacation time the minute he read the article."

"Why?" I asked. "There's not anything he can do about Bretta," I said, my eyes not meeting hers. "It's not his fault she's dead." I muttered. It's mine, I thought, but I didn't say that.

She sighed. "Because the same kind of murder happened here about six years ago. Your father was working that case. It was a young girl about Bretta's age."

I put the bite of pancake back down on the plate. Here was another breakfast that was going to get cold. Mom had my attention. "Who was it?" I asked.

"Her name was Tally. Her mom was a librarian and everyone in town rallied around trying to locate the girl. She went missing one afternoon after school and wasn't found until five days later. The parents were devastated. It was their only daughter, and …"

"Like Bretta," I interrupted.

Mom thought for a second, then nodded. "Yes, like Bretta. Anyway, when her body was found, she'd been beaten. They never found out who did it. It was so sad. Her parents came home one afternoon and found the front door standing open, but nothing was missing—except Tally. After they searched the house and realized she wasn't home, they began noticing things. Her shoes were still by the back door along with her coat. Her snack was on the table half-eaten— things like that." She stopped as if remembering something. "It was about this time of year, I think."

My mind was trying to process all the things Mom was telling me. Another murder. Six years ago. Why hadn't I heard about this? Then I remembered I would have been eight at the time. A murder isn't the kind of thing you share with an eight-year-old kid. Mom was still talking.

"... Then the trail got cold, and it was filed away as an unsolved case.

But your father never forgot," she said, looking out the window. "It ate away at him, and I don't think he ever really forgave himself. He felt responsible for not finding the murderer. I tried to tell him there weren't enough clues. But it didn't help. He started to change.

"For weeks after the killing, he insisted on being the one to tuck you in. It was like he wanted to make sure he could make you safe. He used to stay in your room for hours just watching you sleep." Mom took a deep breath. "And then the accident happened, and that seemed to push him over the edge" Her eyes were focused on me. "After that, he started pulling away from us. He quit going to church. He stopped coming home on time. The accident was like the final thing that changed him."

"The accident?" I asked, not meeting her gaze.

"The accident," she replied, raising my chin. She raised one eyebrow. "And don't try to act innocent. It never works. I know you overheard the conversation between Jane and me the other night, Rachel."

"How did you know?" I asked.

"Moms know." She grinned. "It's okay. It's time you understand what really happened."

I sat back and looked at her. "Yeah, I did overhear you two talking. Dad was driving the night Aunt Jane got hurt. Right?" I asked.

She nodded. "When the accident happened, things were just starting to get back to normal for us." She stopped and swallowed hard. I could tell this was going to be hard for her.

"It's okay, Mom. If you don't want to tell me yet, it's okay."

"No, you really do need to know. You must understand your father did *not* walk out on us, Rachel. He had to go away. He had to," she said. She scooted back her chair and walked to the coffeepot. She poured a big mug and came back to the table. I waited as she sat down.

"You okay?" I asked.

"I'm fine. The night the wreck happened, I was at home. You were sick, and I didn't want to leave you. Jane had been working late." She paused. "She used to work at the public library. Did you know that?" I nodded, a memory of Aunt Jane and my first library book flashing in my mind.

"Anyway, she had car trouble. I called your father and asked him to swing by the library and pick her up. He agreed. I knew he'd been in court that afternoon testifying against a man he arrested." She stopped and took a sip of coffee.

"You want me to finish this?" It was Aunt Jane. Mom and I both jumped at the sound of her voice.

"Jane ..." Mom started.

Aunt Jane shook her head. "I'm glad you're telling her." She came over and squeezed my shoulder. "You're not a little girl anymore. I suppose we've treated you as though you were for far too long. Maybe this will explain questions that have been racing around in that intelligent brain of yours." She reached over and took a bite of my pancakes. "Hmm. Blueberry. Got any more?"

"What your mother and I didn't know was that a threat had been made at the end of the trial," she explained. "The man was convicted, and rightly so, of child abuse. Your father was the reason he was going to jail. His evidence, along with his testimony, was enough for the court to find the man guilty. Thank you, Liz," she said, as Mom placed a steaming plate of pancakes in front of her. I slid the syrup and butter toward her.

"Anyway," she continued, "the man's brother was furious. He refused to believe his brother was guilty and told Steve that someone would have to pay for all the damage done to their family. No one gave it much thought. People are spouting that kind of stuff all the time." She took a bite and smiled.

I couldn't believe how calm she was. Whatever happened that night changed her life forever, but here she was, telling me about it and eating blueberry pancakes.

"Well, the brother's idea of 'doing something about it' was to follow your dad out of the parking lot. Steve never noticed him, but another officer did. So, he followed the guy. I forget the brother's name," she said, waving her fork in the air.

"How can you forget his name?" I asked incredulously.

"What good is remembering going to do me?" she asked. "We're supposed to forgive, honey. Holding on to hate doesn't help the forgiving part along."

I shrugged and settled back into my chair. I would have to leave pretty soon, and I did not want to leave this room without hearing the rest of the story.

"I was waiting in front of the library when he pulled up. I got in and buckled up. My apartment was only a few miles away, and I knew it wouldn't take long to get there. I remember thinking it odd that no traffic was on the streets. There wasn't a car in sight. Then, as we approached the first intersection, I noticed a car coming up from my right. There was a car behind him. It was a police car, and he turned his lights on. The light was green for our lane, but Steve didn't accelerate immediately. I'm sure he was waiting to see if the officer would need assistance. We later learned the police officer was your dad's friend, and the car he was following belonged to the brother of the convicted criminal."

"Later, of course, we found out the brother had cut through an alley and was waiting for us to pass by. He had no way of knowing I was in the car, not that it would have made any difference. He just wanted revenge. He probably took great pleasure afterward knowing he'd hurt Steve's relative the way he felt your dad had hurt his brother."

"Are you sure you want to hear this, Rachel?" Mom asked from her seat. She had been sitting quietly for the last several minutes.

"Yeah, of course," I answered. It meant a lot that they felt I was old enough to handle the truth about what happened. There was no way I wanted Aunt Jane to stop now. I turned back to her.

"As we started through the light, the man gunned his engine and headed straight for us. He must have pushed the engine as fast as it would go. I remember hearing the tires make an awful squealing sound. I screamed when I realized he was coming at us." She stopped and dropped her head.

This must be what her nightmares are about, I thought. I looked at Mom, but she was looking at Aunt Jane, concern on her face.

"Jane," Mom said.

"It's okay. I just haven't talked about it in so long it's harder than I thought it would be, that's all." She offered a weak smile and took a sip of water. "Anyway, Steve tried to veer away, but it was too late. The driver hit my side at full speed. My arm was pinned and crushed, and that's why it's paralyzed today. Your father," she said with a grim look on her face, "blames himself. He swears if he had reacted sooner or swerved the car differently, this," she said, pointing to her right arm, "wouldn't have happened. The truth is, if he'd hit us from the back or the front, the accident could have been fatal for both of us. The police officer saw the whole thing and even tried to convince your father that his judgment was not in question. It didn't work."

"Your dad didn't leave because he didn't love us," Aunt Jane said. "It's because he hated seeing a daily reminder of what he feels is his fault. The murder victim's mother and his own sister. The mother wouldn't forgive him and that was a heavy burden.

My therapy didn't progress as we hoped, and Steve and Liz offered to let me move in. If I'd known what it was doing to him, I'd have stayed away. By the time I figured it out, he was gone."

"I didn't know either. I still thought most of it was because of the girl's murder," Mom said, standing and carrying the dishes to the sink. "Now, I think it was a combination. Too much happened that was out of his control, and he turned away when he should have been turning somewhere else."

"Yep. That's about the time he stopped praying," Aunt Jane said. "That's never a smart thing to do. He took the accident hard, but not being able to solve that girl's murder was hard on him too. I haven't thought about that in a long time. Poor Isabel. Losing her little girl nearly killed her. It did kill her husband. He died a few months later."

"I was telling Rachel about that a few minutes ago. It was so sad. I can't remember the girl's last name, though," she said, running water over the dirty dishes. "Do you remember?" Mom asked.

I was already heading toward the den to get my books and coat.

"Sure. It was Bentley. I'm pretty sure her mom teaches at the high school now."

TWELVE

"*M*rs. Bentley's daughter was murdered?" I asked, racing back into the kitchen.

"Bentley," Mom mused. "Of course. I should have made the connection before now. The same Bentley who is your English teacher." She turned to Aunt Jane. "Wasn't she teaching something else when all that happened?"

Aunt Jane nodded. "She was the librarian at the high school. She used to come to the public library to check our collection so she could refer her students to us. We had a much larger budget and could afford a lot more reference books and databases than she could. She used to spend hours there on the weekend. She loved her job."

Mom and I looked at each other. "She doesn't love what she's doing now," I rolled my eyes. "I don't think she likes it at all." I gathered up my stuff while Mom grabbed her keys and shrugged into her coat. We headed to the car.

I stayed pretty much stunned all the way to school. Trying to wrap my head around everything I heard this morning was just plain overwhelming. Not to mention trying to cope with last night. On top of that, I had to face Mrs. Bentley first hour. "You're not going to say anything to Mrs. Bentley about what you've learned, are you? That was a long time ago, and I'm sure she's trying her best to put it all behind her. Losing her daughter was horrible enough, but then to lose her husband, too." Mom sighed. "I can't begin to imagine how anyone would cope with those kinds of losses."

"Mom," I said, cutting my eyes at her. "I'm not going to say anything to Mrs. Bentley. That would be mean. Plus, she already hates me. I wouldn't be helping myself by bringing all that up. And no," I said, guessing her next remark, "I won't tell the others, either."

Mom patted my knee. "You wouldn't intentionally hurt anyone. Sometimes it's hard for parents to realize their children are growing up. I guess I haven't completely accepted the fact you're not a little girl anymore." She paused, watching the traffic. "I'm proud of you. You've had a lot thrown at you lately, and you've handled things really well."

She had no idea how irresponsible her daughter was. How could I tell her about my part in Bretta's death? She, not to mention Aunt Jane and now Dad, would completely lose any trust they had in me. But that was going to change. I would fix things. Somehow.

She let me out at the usual drop-off. Mrs. Doyle was on duty. She waved and gave me a big smile. Confused, I met her as she walked toward me.

"Rachel, I spoke with Mrs. Bentley yesterday afternoon, and you have permission to come to my office as soon as you finish your test this morning. Does that sound okay with you?"

I forgot about my appointment with Mrs. Doyle. Well, it was too late to change things now. She'd gone to the trouble of getting permission. I nodded. "Okay. That's great," I said. "If I can't make it today, I'll be there tomorrow as soon as I can. Thanks, Mrs. Doyle."

The bell rang, and I hurried past the sagging banner bearing Bretta's name and went into the building. When I walked into Mrs. Bentley's class, the first thing I noticed was the happy faces. Everyone was talking and not in whispers. Some were laughing out loud. I backed up to make sure I was in the right classroom. Mrs. Bentley's name was stenciled on the outside of the room. I stepped back in. Pam motioned me over.

"Can you believe this?" she asked excitedly. "Mrs. Bentley's not here today. We're going to have a sub. Isn't that great," she said, dancing in her seat.

"Yeah, great," I repeated. I dropped my books on my desk. I turned back to Pam. "So what's wrong with Mrs. Bentley?" I asked.

"Who knows? Who cares? I'm just glad she's not here."

I wanted to tell Pam what I knew. It might make a difference in the way a lot of the kids looked at the teacher. Maybe she wasn't really such a monster after all. Mom was right. Losing your kid and your husband all in the same year would be hard.

But I wouldn't tell Pam. I wouldn't tell anyone. I'd journal how I felt about all this, but that would be as far as it went. I promised Mom, and I didn't want to lose her trust. Instead, I told Pam about meeting with Mrs. Doyle. I also told her about my Dad being back, but she didn't seem surprised.

"That's great," she said, smiling. "Don't you get it? He was worried about you or he wouldn't have come back. I think it shows he really cares, Rachel," she said. "Did you tell them about the van?"

I nodded. "Yeah, I told them. The police said there's been a bunch of break-ins in the neighborhood. They think maybe the van is involved."

Pam nodded, then turned in her seat as the door opened. Mr. Jennings stepped into the room, a stack of papers in his hand. He looked flustered.

"Class," he began. "Mrs. Bentley is out sick today. I will be handing out an additional study guide for you to go over to get you ready for the test tomorrow. He stopped shuffling the papers and looked up. Evidently, he expected the room to come alive with moans at the mention of the test. But no one was complaining at all.

When he started handing out the papers, I picked up my pencil and looked around the room. Someone else was missing, too. Billy

Isley. I wasn't surprised. I figured he'd skip today. I was sure he'd overheard my conversation with Pam about study night and then thought up a way to get Mom and Aunt Jane out of the house. Maybe he wasn't as dim as I thought. Either that, or he had help. That would explain how he could be stealing the notes while somebody else drove that van.

I couldn't believe how stupid I'd been. Why hadn't I been more careful about keeping the notebook with me? Now I only had the copy. I was positive the original was gone by now. Probably up in smoke. At least he didn't know about the copy, and I wasn't about to tell him.

What if Billy was Bretta's murderer? What would he have done to make sure no one else saw that notebook?

I didn't have to worry about that now. He had the notebook. In Billy's mind, he probably saw that as the answer to his problems. If I couldn't prove he had a link to Bretta, he wouldn't worry about me.

I took the study guide Mr. Jennings held out to me and wrote my name, homeroom, and date on the paper, and then turned it over to study the questions. It was laid out pretty much the same way as one of the trial tests we ran off at Pam's house using the test maker website. Starting at the top, I worked my way down and discovered something great. I knew most of the answers. After last night, I worried maybe I wouldn't remember much from my study time with Pam and the others. But after twenty minutes I was proofing my guide. When I looked up Mr. Jennings was smiling at me. He motioned me to the front.

"I understand Mrs. Doyle would like to speak with you," he said, nodding toward the door. I nodded, too, turning in my guide. I went to get my things. Pam and the others were concentrating on their guides. I slipped out the door and headed down the hall. It was quiet. Most people were in the middle of their first period classes. I hoped I'd be able to finish with Mrs. Doyle and make it to second period on time. I didn't want to have to borrow anyone's notes.

Mrs. Doyle met me at the door, smiling. She was carrying a mug in her hand and motioned for me to go into her private office. As I went through the outer area this time, I took the time to really look at the way she had it set up.

She noticed my gaze. "Do you like this room?" she asked.

"It's great," I said. "It makes it feel homey in here."

"That's what I was going for. I want everybody who comes in here to feel comfortable. Sometimes people just need a place to go to hang out for a while."

I nodded and smiled at her. "You did a great job," I said. "I really like it."

"Thanks," she beamed. "I'll be right back," she said, waving her coffee mug. "I have to get another cup of caffeine. For some reason, I'm having a hard time waking up today." I smiled and went into her office, sitting in the same chair as I had on Monday. I wasn't feeling the panic I felt then. While I hadn't come to grips with Bretta's death, at least now I had a goal. I knew I was partly responsible for her death, and I was determined to do something to make up for it.

"Okay," Mrs. Doyle said, hurrying in the door a few minutes later. "I'm sorry, Rachel," she said, plopping down in a chair. "Some days require a jumpstart." She lifted her mug. "I guess this is one of those days. So how are you doing?" she asked, tucking one leg under her.

"I'm better," I said. "I was having a bad day yesterday, but I'm better now."

She leaned forward. "I didn't know yesterday was so difficult. Was Bretta on your mind?"

"No, it wasn't Bretta. Well, not exactly," I said, deciding to tell her about the dream. "I had a really bad nightmare the other night after Bretta's parents came to the house." I chose my words carefully. I didn't want the wrong information slipping out. Leaning back into the chair, I went on. "After they left, I was upset so I went to bed. When I woke, Mom and Aunt Jane were with me."

She looked concerned. "Why were the Deevers at your home?"

"They brough some stuff of mine I left at Bretta's," I answered, hoping she wasn't going to ask what those things were. My mind raced to the notebook with the notes between Bretta and Billy. But another thought was resting just out of reach. Something I had missed. It wasn't the loss of the notebook. There was something else that I should have caught. Mrs. Doyle was asking me a question. "I'm sorry," I said. "What did you say?"

She nodded and took a sip of coffee. "Do you remember the dream?"

I looked away. "No," I lied. I did remember the dream. It wasn't as vivid as that night, but I could still see Bretta's eyes staring into mine.

"I know dreams can feel so real. One of my brothers has recently started having horrible dreams, and my mom isn't sure what to do. I told her to let them run their course. Pretty soon, when he's dealt with whatever it is he's worried about, the nightmares will go away. I suspect the same thing will happen to you. I'm not saying it will be easy to get over Bretta's death, but time really is a great healer. My mom used to say that all the time, and I thought it sounded so lame. Now, I realize she was right."

"I hope so," I said, looking at my hands. And I did. More than anything, I wanted to believe that once I did something to make up for my horrible choice, the bad dreams, the guilt, and even some of the bad memories would go away. I looked at my watch. We'd been talking for almost fifteen minutes, and I still hadn't mentioned the reason I made the appointment with her in the first place. It didn't seem as important as it had yesterday, but I still thought it might be nice to hear her advice about my dad. I was opening my mouth when we both heard running footsteps coming down the hall. Even with the outer door closed, the sound was loud. They stopped right outside her door.

Mrs. Doyle stood and went to the outer door. I stayed in my seat and waited for her. But then I heard the door swing open, and she gave a yelp, like the door had hit her. I was dying of curiosity, but before I had a chance to go to the door and peek out, she appeared in the doorway. She was frowning.

I wanted to ask her who the rude kid was, but I knew she wouldn't tell me. Mrs. Doyle won't talk to students about other students.

Now, she was trying to smile and look calm, but this time the grin she put on didn't look sincere. It looked like she was trying really hard to smile. "Rachel, I'm sorry. I have an emergency, and I'll be with you in just one minute, I promise." She pulled the door almost shut, but like most of the doors in the old school, it had a mind of its own. It swung open about two inches. Should I try to sneak a peek at who was in the other room? I could hear voices. They were whispering.

I strained my ears to make out the sounds. One was a boy's voice. It was hard to identify because he was talking in a low whisper. I caught the word *note* and *excuse,* but that was all. I heard Mrs. Doyle sigh and then heard scribbling sounds. There was a tearing noise, like she ripped a piece of paper from a pad. Then clearly—very clearly, I heard the boy's voice. This time he didn't bother to whisper. I knew immediately who the voice belonged to.

"Thanks, Sis. I owe you one." It belonged to Billy Isley.

THIRTEEN

I knew I was now the one being rude but couldn't help it. The need to know was huge. The minute she reentered the office, I turned and blurted out, "Billy Isley is your brother?" I searched her face, hoping she'd burst out laughing. Instead, she shrugged and offered me a weak grin. Then she nodded. I fell back into the chair.

"He is," she said, sighing. "He's lived with our father out west for years, and now," she said, wrapping her slender hands around her coffee mug, "he's come to live with Mom."

She didn't have to give me details. I got it. One parent gets tired of their kid, so they send them off to the other parent for a while. It was pretty clear from the look on Mrs. Doyle's face that this is what had happened to Billy. I knew she wouldn't give me any details, especially any that happened to be about her brother. When the second period bell rang I think we were both relieved.

I stood. "Thanks for listening," I said. "I really appreciate it."

"Are you sure there's nothing else you wanted to talk to me about, Rachel?" she asked. But I could tell her mind was somewhere else. Probably on her brother.

"No. I'm really doing a lot better. Thanks." I left her office and zigzagged my way through the outer area. I hadn't told her anything about Dad, but that was okay. After the talk I had with Mom and Aunt

Jane this morning, I didn't resent Dad being home as much anymore.

After all, Dad was still dealing with his own blame. Was that why he'd come home? I thought about that for a second. No. I didn't think so. He came home to make sure I was okay. I was pretty sure he still felt guilty, and he probably wanted to do something about it, but wasn't that the same thing I was doing? But I wouldn't run away from the problem like he had. That had been his mistake. He ran away. I couldn't do that. No, it was better to deal with it, and that's what I planned to do. I was determined to help catch Bretta's killer, and Billy Isley was a strong suspect. It bothered me that Mrs. Doyle could be hurt, but I couldn't help that. If he'd done it once, he might do it again. And she said her brother was having nightmares. Was it about the murder? Billy didn't really seem the type who would stress over a stranger's death—unless he had something to do with it.

Something else bothered me. Why go to all the trouble of assuming another identity in the chat room. Why didn't he just set up a date with her? I thought about that while I walked down the hall. Then it hit me. He was afraid he couldn't trust her not to tell someone she was meeting him. Plus, she might have said no. Since she'd already broken it off with him, why waste her time?

Heading for my locker, I noticed Harvey at the end of the hall. He looked up and smiled, looking so much like a sweet old basset hound that it made me smile. Reaching into the machine, he pulled out a bottle of peach juice, but I shook my head.

"Nope, not today, Harvey," I twirled my combination number and opened my locker, getting out my history book and throwing my lit book inside. Then I turned back to him. "Harvey," I said, looking around. The hallway was busy. Everyone was talking. I moved closer so only Harvey could hear my words.

He looked up, surprised. "You change your mind?" he asked, again reaching inside the machine.

"No," I answered. I checked again for anyone who might overhear our conversation. "Harvey, didn't you tell me your little brother died?"

His face changed from smiling to sad. "Yeah," he said, ducking his head. "He was a little kid when it happened. We were playing ball." He rubbed his chest with the palm of his hand, but stopped when he noticed me looking. "Sometimes, my old ticker acts up. Anyway," he explained, "I threw the ball too hard, and it bounced into the street. A car was coming. I watched him go down."

"Did they catch who did it?" I asked.

He shook his head. "No. The car never even slowed down."

"What did you do?" I asked.

"I rushed out there and dragged Kenny out of the street. I didn't know you weren't supposed to move somebody when they'd been hurt like that, you know? All I could think of was to run and get him out of the street. Then I tried to wake him so he could stand up." He looked down at the bottle in his hand. He placed it back in the machine and turned away from me. I noticed his shoulders were hunched. All of a sudden, Harvey looked really old. My heart twisted. I knew exactly how he felt.

"I guess he was already dead then. He was so still, but his eyes were open. I didn't understand how his eyes could be open unless he was okay. One of the neighbors came driving by and stopped. I guess she knew right away he was— gone. She ran up the walk to one of the other neighbor's house and called the police and the ambulance. I sat there and held Kenny. The stupid ball I'd thrown had landed a few feet away. I remember staring at that while we waited for the ambulance to get there."

The bell rang, and I was late for class. I didn't care. I wanted to hear what Harvey had to say.

"That's why I know how you're feeling," he said. "It's hard to lose somebody." He looked at me again. Of all the people who tried to help, Harvey was probably the only one who knew exactly what I was feeling. But even he didn't realize how close our situations were. No one knew.

But Harvey felt the same guilt I was feeling. He'd thrown the ball that made his brother go into the street. He must have felt he caused

Kenny's death just like I felt responsible for Bretta's.

"Did you ever want to find out who did it?" I asked, careful not to look in his eyes. I focused on the books in my hands. When he didn't answer immediately, I looked up and found him staring hard into space.

Then in a whisper, he said, "Yes. I sat in our front yard for weeks waiting for that same car to come by. It never did."

"But if you could have found out who was responsible, would you?"

"Of course."

"What would you have done?" I asked.

"I'd have turned him in so he couldn't hurt anybody else," he answered. Then he bent over the stacks of cans, but stopped as he was lifting a crate from the floor. "Why? Why do you want to know all this stuff?" Jerking upright, his eyes grew large as he looked at me. He took a quick step toward me. "No!" he said, shaking his head and frowning. "I know what you're thinking. I felt the same way, but you can't let yourself get involved in this. This is different."

He looked at me for a long time. "No," he repeated. "You use your head. You're a smart girl. Going after a killer isn't something you do. Let the police handle this," he said. He looked around, and even though there was no one else in the hall, he lowered his voice to a whisper. "Whoever did that to your friend could come after you. Don't you know that? You must have thought of that," he said, his voice rising.

It was too soon to share my thoughts with anybody, so I nodded my head and smiled. "You're right, Harvey. I'm just frustrated because the police haven't found the guy yet. Everything they do takes forever."

"I know," he said, but his tone was wary. "But still, they'll find out who did this. Stop worrying. This is different from when Kenny was— killed. That person who hit him probably didn't get up that morning meaning to find some little kid and run him down. Whoever hurt your friend, well, I think whoever did that, meant to." He searched my face. I gave him another smile.

"Don't worry, Harvey. I promise I won't do anything stupid."

He seemed relieved. Picking up another handful of drinks, he inserted them into their slots. "You remember what I said. Okay?"

"Okay." Talking to Harvey helped. At least I knew I wasn't the only one who had ever gone through this.

Now I was almost fifteen minutes late for class. "I have to go, Harvey. Thanks for talking to me," I said, hurrying down the hall. I'd go to the office and get a tardy excuse for Mr. Peterson. I was pretty sure they would give one to me without asking too many questions. Everyone, especially the teachers and administrators had been treating me like I might break in two since Monday morning. Now, they would think I'd either been talking to Mrs. Doyle or had gone in the restroom to get myself together.

I felt a little guilty about that, too. It was like lying. It wasn't that I was taking advantage of it. I hadn't stopped to talk just so I could get out of class. I needed to know what Harvey had to say about his brother's death. Still, my conscience tugged at me.

Mrs. Bentley was absent today, but she didn't seem to be too worried about me anyway. Billy Isley sure wasn't. In fact, I'm pretty sure it would be okay with both of them if I fell off the face of the planet. But maybe it wasn't complete hatred on Mrs. Bentley's part. Maybe she turned the whole world off when she lost her family. That would be enough to make most people mad at the world. Bretta's murder must have brought back awful memories. I wondered if that was why she was absent.

I arrived in the office as Mrs. White, the secretary, was making an announcement. "Funeral services for Bretta Deevers will be held Friday morning at 10:00 in the White Chapel. Graveside services will follow at the Lerner Cemetery. Visitors and friends are encouraged to visit the Deevers' home after the graveside services are finished."

When she ended her announcement, she turned and saw me. Her face softened, and I swallowed hard. "I need a tardy slip for Mr.

Peterson's class," I said. I'm sure she saw the tears in my eyes.

She didn't ask for an excuse. Scribbling a note, she passed it to me. I walked out of the office and went to second period with a heavy heart. When I walked in, the class stopped, and I felt like falling through the floor. I hurried over to Mr. Peterson who was standing at his podium and handed him the admit-to-class slip. Then I walked to my seat and took out my book. Glancing at the note, he put it in front of him then continued his lecture. As hard as I tried, I couldn't keep my mind on the subject.

I kept seeing the pain in Harvey's face. After all these years, it still hurt him to talk about his little brother. Is that what it was going to be like for the rest of my life? Would it be different once Bretta's killer was caught? I knew the answer to that. The *only* way my life would improve was if *I was the one* who helped find the killer.

The period finally passed, and the bell rang. I looked forward to the next period. There was something about the library I liked. Being an aide in there was a good part of my day. Today was no different. Mrs. Hernandez always gave each of her helpers a free day. After shelving, we could use the library for whatever we needed. My free day is on Thursday. Usually, I want to read or use some of the special equipment. But today, I wouldn't get on the computer to stream video. I'd be using the computer to dig up information from six years ago. I knew from working in the library that a Google search probably wouldn't give me the kind of articles I was looking for. It wasn't a bad place to start, but for the kind of stuff I wanted, I'd have to go into some of the more advanced databases. All of the aides were trained in using them for when teachers and other students needed hard-to-find articles.

I'd decided I wanted to find out more about the murder of Mrs. Bentley's daughter, Tally. Something about it scared me and interested me at the same time. Maybe it would help me understand Mrs. Bentley. I sure didn't understand much about her now.

After I'd stashed my stuff in the back, I saw that four people were browsing around, and there was no sign of Mrs. Hernandez. Surely she wasn't absent, too. If she was, I'd lose my free day and have to work at the circulation desk plus do my other jobs. I didn't really mind, but I had my heart set on looking up those old articles.

When the last student was checking out, Mrs. Hernandez hurried in the door. Her face was flushed, and she was out of breath.

"Oh, Rachel," she said, hurrying to the desk. "I'm so sorry. We had a slight problem." She took a deep breath and placed both hands on the desk. "I can always count on you," she smiled, "to hold down the fort."

I smiled. "Anything serious?" I asked, stacking the returned books behind me.

"Not really. One of the faculty members is out today, and I had to cover her class for the first few minutes."

I knew she was talking about Mrs. Bentley. Seely High is a small school. News travels at warp speed around here. Mrs. Hernandez had forgotten I have Mrs. Bentley first period. I picked up a stack of books from my section and plopped them onto the wheeled cart. I went into the back room to get some book ends. I heard the outer door open and could hear another voice besides Mrs. Hernandez. It was Mrs. Doyle. I stopped and backed up so they wouldn't see me in the back. Something about the way the two of them had their heads together made me want to hear what they were saying.

"Have you noticed anything odd about Mrs. Bentley lately?" Mrs. Doyle asked. Her voice was very quiet, even though no one else was in the room. I was kind of shocked by her question. I figured teachers kept this kind of conversation in the teacher's lounge.

"She seems a little stressed lately," Mrs. Hernandez said carefully.

"That's it exactly," she said. "Lately, she isn't herself." She tapped her lip with her finger.

"I suspect this situation with Bretta has brought back bad recollections for her."

"What bad recollections," Mrs. Doyle asked innocently.

"Oh, I thought you knew. Everyone's been talking about it," the librarian said quietly. She hesitated a little while, as if she were trying to decide whether to share. I guess she decided it was okay because she went right on talking. "I knew Mr. Jennings spoke with her last Monday to see if she was okay."

So *that* was why he came to the classroom. He'd been worried about *her*. Mrs. Hernandez was still talking. "Several years ago, Mrs. Bentley's daughter was killed. It was an awful ordeal. She and her husband doted on that little girl. They gave that child everything she wanted. Neither one of them made much money, but you wouldn't know it to see how they lavished things on her."

I was surprised by Mrs. Hernandez's description of Mrs. Bentley. It was like she was talking about a totally different woman. Doting. Kind. Generous.

"Then, one day, they came home, and her daughter was gone. Poof." I heard fingers snap. "The police looked for days, and let me tell you, those parents nearly went insane. Why, she was their whole world. I had just started working here then, as Mrs. Bentley's assistant. I was working on my master's degree, but hadn't finished it. I was doing my internship with her when it happened," she explained.

"I've never known anyone to go down as fast as she did. She stopped eating. She lived on coffee. Then when they found Tally— that was the little girl's name, you know," she continued, shaking her head. "I thought Isabel would die. I really think she and her husband believed Tally had just run off for a while. She'd done that once before, but not a single soul but me knew that."

"Anyway," she said, "Tally had gone off to stay with her friend overnight a few months earlier and hadn't bothered to tell either of her parents. They were worried sick, so when they saw she was gone again, they thought she'd taken off to her friend's house. But, of course, they called everyone they could think of, and no one had seen her. They found her snack only half-eaten. Mrs. Bentley blamed herself for letting her go home early without her. She had to stay for a faculty meeting."

I hadn't moved an inch the whole time they'd been talking. My heart was nearly hammering out of my chest.

"Sounds like she had everything a kid could want—probably the newest computers, the newest gadgets. Sometimes, kids can have too much. They need to want for some things." Mrs. Doyle said.

Mrs. Hernandez paused and rubbed her chin. "That child didn't want for anything. They would have moved heaven and earth to get whatever she wanted."

"Do we have any old newspapers with the coverage in them?" she asked.

"Oh, yes!" she said. "They're archived. I keep all the old local newspapers. The major newspapers are all online, and I'm sure Tally's murder was carried in some of them. Anyway, I archive all of our local papers in the back stacks. You're welcome to see them if you like. They're arranged by year."

"Maybe later. I've got to get back to my office. I have a student coming by to talk in a few minutes. Thanks for telling me about Isabel. I knew something was wrong. Now I understand."

I waited until I heard the door close, then wheeled my cart out and had all my books shelved in a few minutes. When I finished, I put my stuff away and went to find the old issues Mrs. Hernandez had talked about. If she caught me, I'd just tell her I'd overheard Mrs. Doyle say she wanted to look at them, and I was getting them for her.

I found the tubs easily. Each one was neatly stacked. But one had been moved out so that the dates weren't in a smooth timeline. When I looked closer, the date showed that it was from papers that were six years old. Somebody else had been back here looking at them! Maybe it had just been Mrs. Hernandez.

It took almost fifteen minutes to locate the first of the articles. It didn't offer any more details than what Aunt Jane and Mrs. Hernandez had talked about. Nothing was ever mentioned about a computer.

Then I scanned the article dated July 15. I couldn't believe what I was seeing. I read, and then reread the words. It made my head spin.

The victim's father, Larry Bentley, a local carpet layer, has

been taken in for questioning regarding the murder of his daughter, Tally. No further details are known at this time.

Her own father? Why did they suspect him? I looked for more details, but there weren't any. There wasn't even another part of the story in later issues. I went back to that last entry.

Was there something I was overlooking? I knew there had to be something else. But what? I read it again, studying each word with care. There it was.

He was a carpet layer.

Then I knew what I'd overlooked the first time I'd read through the article. If he moved and laid carpet for a living, he'd need a long vehicle to deliver it in. He would have needed something like— a van.

FOURTEEN

There were so many similar things about Tally's and Bretta's deaths. Neither had brothers or sisters. Both were girls about the same age. Had Tally arranged to meet someone? And what about the van? That had to be important somehow. These details were too much of a coincidence. I was sure it was important, but none of the articles said anything about a van. But my gut told me it was a clue.

I scanned the rest of the pages, but nothing was reported until the following month. I found an obituary. The article was short and announced the death of Larry Bentley, husband of Isabel Bentley, father of the late Tally Bentley.

He didn't do it, I thought to myself. He loved her with all his heart, and he'd been blamed for her death. He couldn't have done it. No father would do that to his own little girl. Would he?

I blinked a couple of times. Reading about Tally's death made Bretta's death more real. It made it more horrible. And it made me ashamed of my feelings about Mrs. Bentley. She had been through so much hurt. No wonder she didn't want to get close to anyone. I prayed God would help her.

I kept on searching for more information about Tally's death, but the news faded away. One last short article said the investigation had stalled. No more was mentioned, and nothing had been reported about an internet connection of any kind. I hurried out to one of the computers in the library and typed in my database search. The only other articles were from two newspapers that had just rewritten what had been available from the smaller hometown paper. Neither one gave any extra details.

But the question of Mr. Bentley's death nagged at me. The larger newspapers didn't even mention it. I swung away from the computer and went back to the desk. I started to put the tub back in place when Mrs. Hernandez walked in and caught me. If I looked guilty, she didn't say so. She looked at the tub in my arms.

"Just leave it out, Rachel. Mrs. Bentley pulled it. She does that sometimes. It's odd. You'd think she'd want to stay as far away from it as possible. But ..." she shrugged.

I had to hurry so I wouldn't be late for my fourth period class. I didn't want to make a habit of being late.

I had so many questions. I sure couldn't go to Mrs. Bentley. Obviously, Mom and Aunt Jane had either forgotten a lot of the facts, or they never knew them. The newspapers were a dead end. Then I remembered Dad. He'd worked the case! He'd know all the details, even those not given to the reporters. But would he share them with me? Talking him into that might be a problem. But I had to try. Maybe somewhere in all those long-ago clues, I might find something to help solve Bretta's death. I'd become so sure Billy was guilty I'd let myself close out any other possibility. That was dangerous. Maybe it wasn't Billy at all.

That thought was scary. What if it was someone else who had killed Tally *and* Bretta? But six years apart? That was crazy. Once Tally had been killed, that person would have left, wouldn't he?

My mind turned somersaults as I sat down in art class. It was hard to concentrate on the video Mrs. Watson was showing. The topic was perspective, and the one thing I learned from the whole lesson was to look at things from different angles. Talk about making connections to real life!

The rest of the day dragged. I couldn't wait to get home and talk to Dad. It might be hard, but I was sure I could talk him into sharing things about Tally's death. I had to be careful, though. In a lot of ways, he still saw me as that little eight-year-old baby. I wasn't. I'd grown up a lot since he'd left.

I got my chance sooner than I'd expected. Dad was sitting in the pick-up line, waiting for me to exit the building. He was driving Mom's car. My first thought was something might be wrong at the shop. I guess my face looked worried because when I climbed in the car, he reached over and patted my knee.

"You gonna tell me what's wrong?" he asked.

I slumped back against the seat. "What makes you think anything's wrong?"

Because you always get that little worry furrow between your eyebrows when you're fretting about something," he said, watching the traffic. "Even when you were a baby, you had that little dimple up there. Your mother used to call it your worry-wart pucker." He swung left, and we headed home. Hmm. Maybe Mrs. Bentley and I had that in common, too. I just hoped mine didn't begin to look like hers.

This was the first time in six years my dad had picked me up at school. But it didn't feel weird. It felt like the most natural thing in the world. Like it happened every day. Then I caught myself. Yeah, but how long would it last?

"You want to go get some ice cream?" he asked.

I shook my head. "No, I'm not really hungry. Um, how's your head?" I asked, looking at the cut. I didn't even try to be tactful. I turned around in my seat so I could examine it. I was still worried about how hard I hit him. Even with Mom's joke about him having a hard head, I knew she'd been worried about him.

"I'm fine, Kitten," he smiled.

This time I didn't flinch. Didn't even blink. I let the pet name float around in the car. I was enjoying this. I knew better than to get my hopes up, but maybe it wasn't such a bad thing to just enjoy the moment. Right now I wouldn't think any farther ahead than the ride home.

Turning back around in my seat, I tucked one leg under me and decided this was the perfect time to bring up the subject of Tally Bentley's murder. I hadn't really had time to decide just how to do that, so I crossed my fingers and jumped into it.

"Dad, do you remember the kid who was killed about six years ago?" I watched his face carefully. We were sitting at an intersection, and he had his eyes glued to the traffic light. Without taking his eyes away, he nodded.

"Would you tell me about it? There's some things I'd really like to know," I said softly.

He looked at me with a curious stare. Then he shook his head. "No, Rachel. That was a long time ago, and there's no use dredging up the past."

"But I'd like to know, Dad."

"Is this because of what happened to your friend?" he asked.

I nodded. "Yes. They're alike in a lot of ways. Neither of them had brothers or sisters. They both …" I stopped. I'd caught myself just in time. I seriously suspected Tally had hooked up with someone in a chat room just like Bretta had, but that was just a guess on my part, and none of the articles had said anything about it.

"They both what?" he asked. I jumped at the harshness in his voice.

"They both," I hesitated. "They were both about the same age," I said.

He glanced at me and then back at the road. Leaning over, he turned on the radio, which meant the end of the conversation. He wasn't going to make this easy. Neither of us said anything else all the way home. When he pulled into the drive, I unfastened my seat belt and headed for the door. He was close behind.

"Rachel, I don't see what good going over Tally's death would do," he said. His voice was slow. He looked tired. And for the zillionth time this week, I felt guilty. Lately I was always putting people in uncomfortable positions. But I needed answers.

"I understand, Dad. I thought it would help me, that's all." There was surprise on his face like the thought never occurred to him I might need to talk about things. But I did. I needed to talk to him, and not just because I was curious. Now I realized I was a little scared, too. Maybe what had happened to Bretta and Tally could happen to someone else. Dad was quiet as we walked into the house.

All through dinner, which Dad decided would be take-out Chinese, the three adults took turns watching me like they thought I might self-combust. The conversation was forced and there were some things they steered clear of—like Bretta's murder and the service tomorrow.

The meal ended, and everyone went his or her separate way. Dad went for a walk. Aunt Jane went to her room to read, and Mom worked on the computer in her office. Edna and I went upstairs. I put her on the bed and walked to my closet intending to plug in my phone. Then I remembered I didn't have it. I'd lost it the night of the break-in.

My eyes lit on the phone plugged into the charger. It took a second for me to realize whose it was. I stopped and stared. It was Bretta's!

I'd completely forgotten that she'd plugged it in last Friday. Evidently, she had too. Gently, I unplugged it and put it on the floor. It glowed.

What should I do about it? It was evidence. I'd already messed up with the notebook. Should I turn it in? Yes. Should I check her stuff first?

Probably not.

But I was going to. No password required. GREAT!

I went to contacts. There were only two. IB and TG. Who was TG? I scrolled down and went to messaging. I tapped on sent messages hoping she hadn't deleted them. She hadn't. They started with her thank you for the phone. I sat down on the floor and started reading what she'd sent to IB the week before. It read like journal entries.

Wednesday

Thx for my new phone! LOVE it! Ive prolly got the only mom who wont let her kid have a REAL phone. I'm 14, and she treats me like a fifth grader! paraoid and proud of it. makes her think shes a good mom. Shed freak if she knew bout this one. Its awesome!

I searched the inbox, but it didn't have anything. Whoever had sent the phone had enough sense not to send a return text. Either that, or Bretta had cleared them out. I read on.

Thursday

schools dull today. counselor gave me a flier about an art contest coming up. might try that. old man keeling gave a math test which i aced— hardly!

saw HIM today between classes. cute but stupid. cant deal with him anymore. huge mistake. i'm thinking Monday is a good day to dump a guy. never should have gotten friendly with him.

Friday

You are great to talk to. finally! someone who gets me. California! what a great place 2 live. better than this dump. And ur into art!

Saturday

what was i thinking? Left my chat page up while I went to the bathroom today at the coffee house.

i cant believe this guy. he parks in front of MY computer and reads MY stuff! acted all sorry but he took his sweet time when i went over 2 him. DOM. guess thats what i get for not closing down. gotta get better about that. don't want dirty old menreading my stuff. He looked kinda like someone I should know but cant figure it out. gag me.

Monday

love the chat room! can't believe how great it is 2 finally CONNECT w somebody who likes all the same stuff as me. Ur awesome. time 2 get rid of rachel. getting stale. move on and up. maybe i could fix her up with HIM. that would get rid of both my problems and they wouldnt be bugging me all the time.

Wednesday

bored. Whats my surprz you talked about. Tell meeeeee.

CHAT

Friday

Bak at the coffee house. hottie in the house. u should c what just walked in the door. wouldn't tell me his name but i'll get it out of him. likes black coffee. yuk. didn't think ANYBODY drank black coffee anymore. guess he's a rebel. looks the type. kinda like a really hot rocker. hot hot hot. left his phone number! wonder if hes comin back. hope so.

Monday

marvelous mom stone slobberin drunk most of the weekend. stayed in my room all day saturday. dad worked and came home late. went 2 rachels and hung out. such a baby. she likes my art though. at least thats one good thing about her. not completely lame.

Wednesday

okay. Dying to find out about surprz,???

Friday

Think Ill work on my sketch tomorrow for the art contest. i can xpect 2 c THE GUY again tomorrow. i called him yeah i really did it—said he would come in tomorrow if he got a chance and we'd talk. cant wait.

rachel just called my other cell. told her i was busy and couldnt b disturbed. LOL! she believed me. she would. waste of time there. LOTS of time wasted. but she could still come in handy.

Saturday

no sign of THE GUY lately but its reallllllllllllllllly early. Im at the coffee house now. maybe he'll come in and offer 2 drive me home. cant let mom or dad see him so hed have 2 let me out b4 we got home but sure would b nice 2 ride with him. work on sketch now. no one is here. not even regular guy. don't know his name. gotta find out. probably something like joe or hoss or something dorky like that. probably made him mad when i called him nosy. rachel called last night. tried 2 be rude 2 her. don't think she's smart enough 2 get it.

Saturday pm

Gotta talk rachel into covering for me. shouldnt have acted like such a skank with her. now i need her. i think she'll cave. shell jump at the chance. no word from TG yet.

Monday

okay. TG stood me up. that really makes me want 2 get in his face when i see him. i've NEVER been stood up b4. not even cute but stupid did that. my sketch is almost done. its an angel painting a sunset. turned out really cool. used 5 different neutrals and its awesome. Wanna see it got info on art schools in calif. thats what i want 2 do. get out of Podunk away from DM (drunk mom) and LD(lame dad). i'll move 2 Calif and go 2 school. probably hook up with some rich dude get famous with my art and then come back here just 2 show everybody. that will be so sweet.

Wednesday

called rachel last night and asked if we could get together on friday. all i have 2 do is figure out how 2 work her. ive boxed up all her stuff but can't take it 2 her yet b/c she'll know i'm dumping her. i'm really tired of it sitting in my room though. it's in the way. i'll have 2 tell her about you. she'll freak when she finds out. gotta be ready 4 that. i'll just turn it around and make her feel bad about not helping me out. shes a sucker. she'll fall 4 it. she always does. can't wait to meet. its about time!

Friday

she said yes. meet you at the park. Can't wait.

I sat and stared at the phone screen, totally stupid with shock. I couldn't believe what Bretta wrote about me. I reread every entry thinking the words would magically change or something. How could I have been so blind? Getting up, I paced around my room. "Calm down, Rachel," I told myself. This wasn't the Bretta you knew. Was it? I had to admit it to myself. She *could* be selfish and even mean, but sometimes she'd been really kind. And there was her art. She was another person when she worked on her art. I hadn't seen the finished piece for the contest. I wasn't surprised that it was an angel. That was her favorite thing to paint. Kind of ironic.

I sat on the bed and made myself read the entire thing again. And again. By the fourth time, I was calm enough for the words to actually come together. I skimmed over the insults she threw out about me and concentrated on other details. It was all there. She'd told IB way to much about herself. Then set up the meeting. And she had the nerve to call *me* stupid?

No doubt cute but stupid was Billy Isley. She even said she shouldn't have gotten friendly with him. But who was TG—That Guy? He was older. How much older? Twenties? Thirties?

I got up and paced. I hadn't noticed anyone new at the coffee shop. A lot of us went there after school and on weekends but I hadn't seen anybody who looked like a rocker. And that would be hard to miss. Who was the regular dude in the shop she posted about? She nicknamed him Regular Joe. He'd read her posts when she'd gone to the bathroom. I sat on my bed and put my head in my hands. Everything about this was confusing. My heart hurt from the things she wrote. But she was right about one thing. I *had* been stupid. I let her use me way too much. It was easier than making her mad. But I should have stood up to her. I was still guilty.

At least now I understood why so many people had agreed with Andy, though. They saw through her. I saw what I wanted to see.

I decided this was as good a time as any to do some journaling of my own. Sitting crossed-legged on the bed, I started searching for a good H word. Why hadn't I seen this side of Bretta? I thought of all the feelings I felt this last week. Anger at the person who killed her. Now I was angry at Bretta, too. Bretta used me.

But it didn't change my part in this. I was guilty of lying, and it cost Bretta her life. It was more important than ever to clear my conscience. Maybe Bretta hadn't cared about my feelings, but I wasn't Bretta. I care about the people who trust me. I had to make things right—for Bretta and for myself.

I kept searching the pages for the right word. *Hearse* my mind whispered. "No," I said out loud. Then my gaze landed on **Hasten.** I read and reread the definition and knew it was the right word for tonight's entry.

***Hasten:* To move or act with haste; to hurry.**

Friday a.m. 12:25

I know I have to make things right. Maybe if I can get more information from Dad, I can come up with a way to set things straight. There has to be a connection between Tally's death and Bretta's. Sounds silly, but I can feel it.

The door downstairs opened and then closed. Setting the journal beside me, I listened as Dad climbed the stairs. His steps were slow and heavy. The stairs creaked as he climbed them.

I was pretty sure he was heading for his room. Mom had offered it to him for as long as he wanted it. I patted Edna and went to my door, trying to decide what my next move should be with Dad. I had to get some answers, and I knew he wasn't ready to just hand them over. If I pressed him about it, would he leave again?

I peeked out the door just as he reached the landing. Stepping out into the hall, I took a deep breath.

"It wasn't your fault," I said.

It was his turn to flinch. Without a word, he began walking toward his bedroom door. I hurried to him. "Did you hear me, Dad? What happened to that girl wasn't your fault."

He looked even more tired than earlier. For the first time, I noticed the gray in his hair and the droop around his mouth. The sparkling brown eyes I loved so much when I was a little kid looked sad and what was the word—forlorn.

"I didn't do my job, Rachel. I was supposed to prove who did it. That was my job, and I didn't do it," he said. Turning to face me, he shrugged one shoulder. "I failed. I failed that little girl, and I failed her family."

So, he *was* still feeling guilty. "Maybe if you talked about it, it would help, Dad." I knew deep down, he needed to unload the baggage. I wanted to hear it, needed to hear it. I told him so.

He opened his door and stepped in, hesitating in the door.

"Did Tally's father do it?" I demanded. If I couldn't tactfully drag the information out of him, I'd be blunt. He turned to me and smiled. "You've been reading up on it, haven't you?" he asked.

I nodded once. "I looked at some of the old newspaper articles," I confessed. "Do you think he did it? I read where he was a suspect."

"No. He wasn't guilty. He adored that little girl. The newspaper reporters got wind that we'd brought him in for questioning, and they had a field day with it. Rumors started flying and," he drew in a long breath, "it was awful. We still don't know who leaked the news, but the bad publicity devastated him. He worshipped his daughter and would have done anything for her."

"Why did the police question him?" I asked. By this time, Dad was moving across the floor, undoing his tie, and reaching for a hanger. I sat on the edge of the bed and waited for a reply. I wasn't leaving until I had one. This part was very important.

"They found traces of blood in his van," he said.

I knew it. He had driven a van! I cleared my throat. "How did he explain the blood?"

"He said Tally had fallen down their steps one day, and he'd taken her to the doctor. She bled from the cut."

"Was that what happened?"

"I think so. We checked with the doctor, and he confirmed he treated Tally for minor cuts and a sprained ankle. There wasn't a lot of blood in the van, but we were grabbing at straws."

"Dad, you were doing your job. Mom said you worked hard on the case. She was proud of how dedicated you were. You didn't do anything wrong."

"She said that?" he asked. His eyes brightened for just a second. I nodded.

"If you read the articles, Rachel, then you know the rest of it, too."

He sat on the bed beside me. I nodded. "I know he died," I said in a whisper.

"He died three days after the first newspaper article was published. He was found in his shed, honey. He had a massive heart attack."

"You can't blame yourself," I said. "You were just doing your job. If anybody was to blame, it was the newspaper people. You've gotta see that."

He looked down at Edna, who had appeared at our feet. Reaching down, he picked her up and stroked her tiny ears. "I don't know what I believe anymore. I do know that his wife blamed me. After his death, she even phoned the house and told me I was the cause of her husband's death. She swore one day I'd pay for what I'd done. She hated me. Everyone in the department thought she'd move away, especially once she received her husband's life insurance, but she didn't. I still don't understand why she wanted to stay here. Maybe she felt like she was abandoning them if she moved. She's still miserable. You can see it in her face."

"You've seen her?"

"At the store the other day. She stopped dead in the middle of the aisle and stared at me. Then she left her cart and walked out of the store."

"But it wasn't your fault!"

"She held the entire police department responsible. Her life had been shattered. She didn't have anyone left in her whole world except a brother, and he lived off somewhere. She was angry and alone and had to place the guilt with someone. So she chose us. I didn't blame her. I couldn't," he sighed. "I still don't. I thought if I went away for a while, I'd straighten everything out."

"You've been away a long time, Dad," I pointed out.

"Yeah, I know," he said.

"So, did you?"

"Did I what," he asked, startled.

"Did you, you know, straighten things out?"

"No. Not really. There's a lot more than Tally's murder that messed me up. A lot more."

The room was so quiet; I could hear Edna purring in Dad's lap. "I know about the wreck." He turned to look at me, horror on his face. Then he turned and left the room, quietly shutting the door. I stood for a few minutes, hoping he might come back, but he didn't.

I felt sorry for him. He'd been dealing with this all these years just like Aunt Jane still dealt with it in her nightmares. I think I finally understood why he went away. I didn't think it was right, but my anger started to fade. It wasn't gone but faded was better than bright and blaring. In his own way, I thought maybe Dad suffered as much pain as Mrs. Bentley. And now, there had been another murder.

And it had happened to his daughter's best friend. I pulled the journal to my lap and added another line.

I will **hasten** *to make things right. For everyone. It's time.*

FIFTEEN

I watched Friday morning wake up. The sky turned purple, then orange, then finally decided to be blue. How could spring arrive on the day of Bretta's funeral? I rolled over and looked at the clock. It was ten minutes after seven. Looking at the closet, I remembered Bretta's shoes and flung the covers off my bed. I dug in my closet until I found them.

I knew her parents should have them. I understood the shoes should be in Bretta's closet right now, but I couldn't bring myself to turn them over to the Deevers. Not yet. I slipped the shoes on my feet and tied them. They fit perfectly.

I walked around the room, looking at them, studying them. What was that old saying about walking in someone else's shoes? I heard Aunt Jane say it a million times. I stood still, closing my eyes. Then I remembered. I could even hear her voice. "If you want to get to know someone, walk a mile in their shoes."

I snorted. I hadn't known Bretta. I'd only seen the side she wanted me to see—one small slice of Bretta Deever's personality. There was a lot I didn't know—including who had killed her. And I didn't know why. I looked at the shoes like they could give me an answer. The frayed laces and tired soles didn't offer any.

My eyes strayed to my computer. I could still imagine her sitting there a week ago today. I remember how upset I'd been when I found her in a chat room on *my* computer.

I heard footsteps coming up the stairs. Somebody knocked.

"Rachel, are you up?" It was Mom. I looked at my feet and realized I was still wearing Bretta's shoes. I kicked them off under the computer table and hurried to the door.

"I'm up," I said, trying to smile.

Her face searched mine. "You look flushed. Are you sick?"

"Just a little cold. Maybe I'll come downstairs and sit in front of the fire."

"Okay," she said, hesitating at the door. "You want me to wait for you?"

"No. I'll be there in a minute. Thanks, though."

"Okay," she repeated, looking at me with those microscopic mom eyes. "Dad and Aunt Jane are already up. You feel like some breakfast?"

"Not really. Maybe a little juice."

She nodded. With another worried glance, she headed down.

When I reached the bottom of the stairs, I could hear the others in the kitchen. I sat on the couch. Edna leaped into my lap and circled twice before settling down. I stared at the fire.

What should I do about the phone? For now, it was back in the closet, hidden. If I turned it over to the police, could they trace it to IB? I knew the answer was probably yes, but I didn't want to turn it over to them. Not yet. I wanted to find out more.

"Rachel." It was Dad's voice. He walked into the den and perched on the edge of the couch. Edna lifted her head, but when no one offered to scratch her ears, she put it back down, snuggling deeper.

"How are you?" he asked. Mom must have told him to come and talk to me. Maybe I was starting to question myself. Or maybe it was a weakness. But a huge part of my heart was shouting to me I should tell him what I'd found out. Plus, what I already knew. Maybe I'd been wrong in not telling the police about Bretta and her involvement in the chat room. Maybe I couldn't catch this person by myself. Dad would understand, plus he'd be able to relate to the way I felt. He'd understand the guilt. I realized he was talking to me.

"Rachel," he said. "This is going to be a hard day to get through. But we'll be right beside you. Okay?" He patted me on the shoulder.

I nodded. "Dad, there's something I really need to tell you," I said, turning to face him. He nodded solemnly, and patted me on the shoulder again.

"I've been thinking about Bretta's death."

"That's understandable. She was your friend."

"I know, but that's not exactly what I meant. I've been thinking a lot about Tally's death, too. Did Tally have a computer? Because I sort of have a theory, and I think maybe …" but I didn't get to finish my sentence.

He stood so suddenly he startled Edna. Jumping from my lap, she hissed at him and ran into the kitchen. "That's absurd, Rachel," he said harshly. "Not only is it childish to think you could possibly find something the entire police department missed, it's also ridiculous and arrogant. Leave the theories to the police department. They'll find Bretta's killer. They don't need help from a teenager."

"You mean like they found Tally's killer?" I asked. I regretted the words the minute they were out of my mouth, but there was no taking them back. Dad's shoulders slumped, and he started to turn away from me then stopped.

"I should never have shared that information with you about Tally's death. I put ideas in your head. But the fact remains, there's nothing you can do to advance this investigation. You're just a kid, Rachel."

He might as well have slapped me. His words hung; suspended like an invisible whip, ready to rip the air between us again. Stuffing his hands in his pockets he walked to the fireplace. I couldn't move. Couldn't even breathe.

He thought I was childish.

I dropped my head, not wanting to look at him. My heart ached. Childish.

Without another word, I headed to the stairs. Once I reached the top, I looked back. He was closer to the fire. I could see his clenched fists. Opening my door, I slid onto my bed. I couldn't believe the way he spoke to me. It wasn't long before Mom was knocking on my door again, a glass of juice in her hand.

"Here. You have to have something on your stomach." She stood beside me as I took the juice. "Are you sure you don't want anything to eat?"

"I'm sure, Mom."

"Your father went out for a while. I'm not sure why," she said, frowning. "I guess this brings back a lot of memories." She sat beside me. Apparently, she hadn't heard Dad's explosion. I caught my breath. We were both facing the computer. Bretta's shoes were in plain sight under the desk.

"Thanks for the juice, Mom."

"You're welcome. I guess we should start getting ready for the service pretty soon." She stood and headed for the door. She hadn't noticed the shoes. "Let me know if you need anything, sweetheart." She paused at the door, her hand on the doorknob.

"What is it, Mom?"

She shook herself. "Oh, I don't know," she said. "The look on your father's face when he said he was going out seemed odd," she said, twisting a strand of her hair. She shrugged. "I'll see you downstairs."

"Okay. I'll be down in a little while." She closed the door, and I jumped up and grabbed the shoes, stuffing them back into my closet. I stared at Bretta's cell phone. The edge of it peeked out from beneath a pajama top. I would NOT share my plan with Dad. I would prove I was not being childish. I'd get someone to help me with this, but it wouldn't be him.

By 9:00, I was dressed and sitting in the kitchen. Aunt Jane was sitting beside me. Mom finished a casserole she planned to take to the Deevers' after the services. Dad was nowhere around. Maybe he'd left again. That was okay.

But then the back door opened, and he walked in. With a quick glance my way, he walked over to Aunt Jane, leaning over to whisper in her ear. She smiled at him, her face lighting up. It was obvious she was beyond happy to have her brother back. I wondered if her nightmares would end now. Or would they get worse?

We had almost seemed like a family again. But not now. I couldn't welcome him. Not yet. His words rang in my ears. Childish. They stung— and they would for a long time.

SIXTEEN

We got to the chapel exactly fifteen minutes before the funeral was supposed to start. My knees were wobbly, and there was a knot in my stomach. I'd never been to a funeral before. It didn't seem right that my first one should be Bretta's. I walked between Mom and Aunt Jane into the sanctuary. Dad parked the car, promising to find us inside. We were supposed to save a seat for him. I would make a point of staying between Mom and Aunt Jane, staying as far away from Dad as possible.

The room we walked into was large, dark, and full of people. We hesitated in the doorway, and an older man appeared at our side. He was dressed totally in black and even had black hair and a starched-looking black hanky poking out of his pocket.

"I believe there are some seats to your right," he whispered. His hand made a sweeping motion, like he was ushering us to a theater production. His face, however, was grim and sympathetic. We settled into the long pew, and Aunt Jane slid down enough for Dad to squeeze in, which he did a few minutes later. He pretended to be examining a spot on the floor, but I knew he was glancing at me. I refused to look at him, instead staring toward the front. Finally, he settled back against the bench.

Bretta's coffin was closed. A huge arrangement of flowers lay on top of the lid. Dozens and dozens of roses filled the room with their heavy smell. There were flowers on stands, in pots, on trellis-looking things, and even on the floor. Near the head of Bretta's coffin, on an easel, was an enlarged poster of one of her art pieces. It was of an angel painting a sunset. This must have been the one she painted for the contest. She had worked five neutral shades in the angel's robe, but the sunset was full of hundreds of brilliant colors. An expensive gold frame showcased the piece.

Someone's cell phone went off, and I jumped. I remembered Bretta's sitting in the closet. I dragged my mind back to the Bretta I'd known.

One time, when I told Bretta how great her art was, she said she liked to paint things the way they should be, not the way they were. I didn't understand what she was talking about then, but now, I think I do. Bretta wasn't perfect. But she loved to create perfection with her paintbrush. Beautiful perfection. I'm not sure what caused Bretta to forget that beauty in herself, but she sure had known how to put it on a canvas.

I closed my eyes as tears slid down my cheek. Aunt Jane reached over and patted my hand. I squeezed hers and felt more tears threatening to follow.

Bretta was in that box. I'd never talk to her again. I'd never have the chance to tell her how much her words had hurt or how glad I was that she was around when Dad had left. I'd never see her again. *She. Was. Dead.* I dug in my pocket for a tissue. The tears were falling all over my face now. Mom shoved a handful of tissues in my hand then put her arm around me. I saw Dad lean forward again. He started to reach out, and then stopped. I saw his hand drop back into his lap. I wondered if he thought I was being childish again. Was he thinking I should buck up and be strong through this? I was going to disappoint him again. Strong was the last thing I was feeling right now. Lonely, guilty and responsible— yes.

The organist began playing, and I jumped. Someone was singing a song I didn't recognize. Next, the organist played Amazing Grace, which I really liked. I was pretty sure Bretta would have liked it, too.

For the next twenty minutes, the minister talked about Bretta. He said nice words about her life and her talents. He talked about her love of art and how lucky the world had been that she had been a part of it. Quiet crying could be heard throughout the whole service. I saw Mrs. Deevers on the front row. Mr. Deevers had his arm around her shoulder. He was wiping tears from his eyes too. I couldn't watch them for long. My heart wanted to rip apart.

Then it was over.

We were walking out of the funeral home and going to our cars. The sun had gone away, and a cold wind whipped at our coats.

"Wait here. I'll bring the car around," Dad said, as he hurried out. Some people were already leaving the parking lot. Others, like us, were getting their vehicles in line to go with Bretta to the cemetery.

Looking at the sky, I saw dark storm clouds gathering. I desperately wanted the rain to wait until Bretta was buried. "Please don't let it rain, yet," I prayed.

"C'mon," Mom touched my arm. "Dad's motioning for us to come to the car. I guess that's our place in line."

I followed and crawled into the back seat with Aunt Jane. I knew they were worried about me, but I couldn't open my mouth. I knew I'd start bawling like a baby. And besides, there weren't any words left—just tears. Lots and lots of tears. I shivered, and Aunt Jane pulled me to her.

"The line's moving," my father announced. I caught him looking at me in the rearview mirror. I refused to look at him, instead looking through the windshield. There were five cars in front of us. The first was the hearse, carrying Bretta. Her parents were in a big black limousine behind her. I didn't recognize the other cars or who was in them. Looking behind us, I saw a half dozen vehicles. The graveside service would be short.

Since the cemetery was only a few miles away, the drive didn't take long. I wasn't surprised to see that oncoming cars were pulling to the side to wait for the funeral procession to pass. A lot of the men in the cars took off their hats. Some bowed their heads. I hadn't really thought about this Southern tradition before. It was a nice thing for people to do.

As the line of cars stopped in the cemetery lane, we were one of the first to get out. There seemed to be a problem in Bretta's parents' car. Mr. Deevers had stepped from the car, but he couldn't get Mrs. Deevers out. I could hear her crying even with the wind whipping around us. Her sobs were horrible. Her life would never be the same. Just like Mrs. Bentley's had changed. Now the Deever couple would suffer as long as they lived. Maybe a part of them had died with Bretta.

I wanted to put my hands over my ears. Instead, I turned my head, looking at the cars behind us. People were crawling out of them and walking toward the gravesite. I was glad to see Mr. Jennings and Mrs. Doyle. I was also glad that her brother wasn't with her.

There was no sign of Mrs. Bentley, either. I hadn't expected her to be here. She'd buried enough people in her life. Pam Nichols and her family were in one of the last cars. A lot of kids had come to Bretta's funeral, but I guess most chose not to come.

I smiled at Pam as she came up to the car. "This has to be tough for you," she said, hugging me. She pulled a phone out of her pocket. "Mom found your phone under my bed at the house when she vacuumed yesterday. I guess it fell out when we tossed everything on the bed." She handed it to me. "The battery will have to be recharged," she whispered.

I nodded. I didn't trust myself to talk, not even to say thank you. I was grateful. I was sure I'd lost it while running from the van but I couldn't tell her now. I couldn't say anything right now. Instead, I grabbed her arm and held on. She understood and started walking with me. We arrived at the grave the same time as Mr. and Mrs. Deevers. She looked even worse than she had at the house. She started toward the casket, her hand held out, but her husband stopped her. She gazed up at him and cried out—a heart wrenching sob that made everyone drop his or her gaze. Everyone but me. I watched as she shook her head, looking confused. After a few minutes the same usher who helped us locate seats in the funeral home placed his hand under Mrs. Deevers' elbow and steered her to a chair on the front. Two rows of folding chairs had been set near the casket. Mr. Deevers helped guide his wife and then sat with her, holding her hand. The minister was standing to the side, waiting for people to settle in.

I didn't think I could make it through the rest of the service without caving. I knew I had to focus on something besides Bretta's casket, so I looked at the people I didn't recognize. They were sitting in the chairs under the tent. I decided those must be family members. Looking around, I saw Mr. Keely behind me. He nodded and placed his hand on my shoulder. Beside him stood Harvey. Others from the school were scattered around. Mrs. White stood beside Mr. Jennings.

The service was all over in less than ten minutes. But not for me. I made my way to Bretta's casket before they lowered it. Leaning over it, so no one else could hear, I prayed for her. I also made her a promise. Then I went straight to the car and got in. Not one word was uttered on the way home. Dad watched the road. Mom and Aunt Jane watched me. I stared out the window.

I knew what I had to do, and as soon as everyone was asleep tonight, I'd do it. I promised Bretta. And this was one promise I intended to keep. No matter what.

The afternoon passed fast. I kept busy by cleaning my room and helping in the kitchen, but my mind was somewhere else. Mom and Aunt Jane delivered the casserole to the Deevers. They hadn't asked me to go, and I was glad. Dad had been quiet all afternoon, choosing to spend time alone in the spare room. Now, I was wandering around the house looking for Edna and thinking about Mrs. Bentley. I wondered if she had a pet. Did she have anyone or anything in her life to care about? What sort of a day had she had? What was she feeling? Was she thinking about Tally? There were so many coincidences. Had she realized the likenesses in both girls' deaths?

I went to the den and walked over to Mom's computer. I entered

Mrs. Bentley's name. I needed to find out where she lived. Only one Bentley lived in Seely so the info popped up fast. She lived on Hanover Drive. Only three blocks away! I had no idea she lived so close.

Sitting back in my chair, I started to think. Mom and Aunt Jane decided cooking would be a good therapy for tonight. They had left fifteen minutes ago to run to the neighboring town to pick up ingredients for a new Thai recipe they read about in a magazine. I took a quick look at the clock. They would get there in about twenty minutes, fifteen minutes to shop, and would need about twenty to get back. Only Dad and I were home, and he was in his room. Besides, I was pretty sure he didn't want to talk to me. If I was quiet enough, he'd never know I was gone. He probably didn't care. I threw on my jacket and slipped out the front door. It took only a few minutes to jog three blocks.

Mrs. Bentley's car wasn't there. But maybe it was in the garage. I didn't think so. I guessed she was visiting Tally's grave. I wondered when she would get back. Maybe she had a meeting. Teachers always had to go to some meeting, even on weekends. I looked up and down the street before hurrying to the garage.

The large metal door was down, but there was a window on the side of the garage. I peeked inside. There was an area wide enough for two vehicles. Mrs. Bentley could easily park her car inside, but it wasn't there. Something else was parked inside. It was big and old.

And it was a van.

SEVENTEEN

By 11:00 p.m. Friday night every light in our house was off. I was pretty sure that everyone, including Edna was asleep. Since the electricity had been turned back on, the house wasn't as cold, but I was still chilled when I slid out of bed and walked to my closet. For a long time, I listened to the house noises. When nothing weird sounded, I took a deep breath and walked to the back of the closet and retrieved Bretta's phone. Deep breath. Sitting on the floor of my closet, I punched the button and looked for the symbol that would tell me if it still had service.

It did. IB had not turned off the service yet? Why? I was relieved, but if IB was the killer, had he just forgotten, or did that mean that IB wasn't the killer and may not know?

Please, God. Let me do the right thing. I wanted to go back in time and tell Bretta I would *not* help her—that I would tell her parents if she decided to meet her internet friend. But I couldn't do that. It was too late. I hadn't wanted Bretta mad at me, and because of that, I hadn't stood up to her. I should have been stronger—more assertive. That was it. I should have been more assertive. Closing my eyes, I saw the face of her mother float in front of me. The sound of her pitiful cry at the cemetery sounded in my ears like it was happening all over again.

I made Bretta a promise today, and I had to keep it. Not just for

Bretta, but for me, too. The guilt was lodged, and it wouldn't shake loose. I tried to talk to Dad. Huge mistake. I wouldn't make that mistake again.

Looking at the time on Bretta's cell phone, I realized I'd been sitting there for almost ten minutes. My fingers were cold. It was time to do something before I lost my nerve. I went to messaging and typed.

Why did you do it?

I sent the text to IB's contact number.

I waited.

Somebody was going to get a surprise when they read a message from a dead girl.

I was pretty sure that person was Mrs. Bentley. Isabel Bentley. IB

When I saw the van in her garage this afternoon, everything clicked. Her husband had driven a van. She kept it all these years. What if she was the person who *had* murdered her own daughter? Dad said *Mr*. Bentley worshipped Tally. What if Mrs. Bentley resented that relationship?

Maybe the blood in the van hadn't been there because of some little accident. What if Mrs. Bentley used it to move her daughter's body to a place where the suspicion wouldn't be on her?

Could she have killed her husband, too? The reports said he died of a heart attack. But how well did they check his body after his death? It was possible that in the middle of all that had happened, the police shied away from doing an autopsy. That meant she would get away with murder. Twice! Her daughter and her husband.

And unless I did something, she might get away with it again. I scooted against the wall and waited, staring at the cell phone in my hand, wishing it would light up with a reply.

But it didn't.

Getting up, I stretched and walked over to the window. The wind was still blowing, and the rain puddled across the yard. But at least it waited until late afternoon to begin. I shivered when I put my forehead on the frosted window. I looked out into the darkness and thought of Tally and how her father must have grieved for her. And then to have been accused of her murder.

But I couldn't figure out why Mrs. Bentley would keep the van all these years. Had she planned to use it again? Maybe she used it on someone else. Bretta? Some other unsuspecting internet kid?

Maybe she just liked to be reminded of what she'd done.

Beep.

A rattlesnake bite couldn't have startled me more.

"Who are you?" Bentley wasn't wasting any time.

"A friend of Bretta's." My hands were shaking so badly I was having trouble punching the right letters. I took a deep breath. **"Why did you kill her?"**

"I didn't kill her. I would never hurt anyone."

"Why should I believe you? She was going to meet you, and now she's dead."

There was a long pause.

"But I didn't do it. She was dead when I got there."

"Were your parents with you?"

Pause.

"No. They dropped me off and went to get some stuff for us to eat."

"Why should I believe you? Why haven't you told anyone?"

"The same reason you haven't gone to the police. And I know you haven't or the police wouldn't still be asking people for information."

I frowned. It was true. Only a few days ago I'd been terrified of getting in trouble. Now, I was sure it was Bentley. Only someone close would know what I was or wasn't doing. I took a deep breath. **"If you didn't kill her, then who did?"**

"I don't know. When my folks dropped me off, I went to find her. She told me where she'd be. I was walking down the sidewalk when I saw Bretta and another person. She was being hit over and over until she fell to the ground. I hid

behind a bush, and when the person finally left, I ran back toward the road. I know I should have gone to check on her, but I was afraid. I was a coward, and I guess I still am. I don't want to get involved."

I lowered my fingers over the keypad. **"Too late. You're way involved. I want to meet you."**

Another long pause. I sat, biting my lower lip, afraid IB would go away. Then words started spreading along the page again.

"I don't want to do that. How do I know I can trust you?"

What a laugh!

"Same here. If you don't come, I'll go to the police. Someone killed my friend, and I'm *going* to find out who did it. Now, will you meet me or not?"

Pause.

"Okay, but it will have to be quick. My folks and I are going back to California Tuesday morning."

This time I paused. But not for long.

"Then we'll meet Monday afternoon—after school. How do I know what you look like?"

"I'm short with blond hair, and I'm a little on the chubby side. My mom is always riding me about losing weight."

Bretta would NEVER have chosen a friend who was overweight. She was always saying tacky things about girls she thought were too fat. This was Bentley. And she was good.

"Where do you want to meet?"

Pause.

"I don't know much about your town. We're visiting my mom's friend, so you tell me, and I'll ask for directions."

I had to think about a place that would be secluded, but safe. A place she'd feel comfortable in, where she would blend in and not feel threatened.

"We'll meet at school."

"Okay. I think I can find that."

"Meet me under the bleachers on the football field. I'll

wait for you. I want to hear exactly what happened."

"**Okay. I can be there around seven o'clock that night. Is that okay? I'll tell you exactly what I saw.**" Pause. "**I'm really sorry about your friend. You will come alone, won't you?**"

There it was. I'd been waiting for this. She wanted no witnesses when she met me. And I knew why. I had a feeling she planned to do to me what she'd done to Bretta. Well, she'd get a surprise.

"**Of course. But aren't you afraid to meet me alone?**"

A long pause.

"**Kind of. But I want this to be over. I'll see you at seven o'clock.**"

I waited for twenty minutes to see if there would be another message. Then I tucked Bretta's phone back into the back of the closet. I felt relieved and terrified.

Of course, she wasn't afraid to meet me. But I should be a little afraid of meeting her. And I was. I knew I had to have help, or it was totally possible that I could become her next victim.

Pulling my journal from my desk drawer, I walked to the bed and gathered up my writing stuff then started flipping through the dictionary until I reached the I section. After a few minutes of searching, I found *Inconceivable*: **unimaginable; unthinkable.**

It was the perfect word for what had happened to Bretta. Bending over the blank page, I began to write.

Saturday a.m. 12:02

I can't go to the police until I have REAL proof. Even Dad won't listen to me. He thinks I'm childish, but he's wrong. He wants to believe the police will catch this killer, but they didn't when Tally was killed. Is it the same person? I think so. It's Bentley.

She has to pay.
*Is it **inconceivable** that I could do this alone?*
Yes.

*Is it **inconceivable** that the killer might kill again?*
No.

I need help.

I stopped writing and frowned. So, who was I going to get to help me? My choices were pretty limited. Mrs. Doyle? Maybe, but she would probably want to tell my parents. She might even tell her brother, and that would really complicate things if he turned out to BE the killer. I really needed someone older, someone I could trust.

Then it came to me. I knew exactly who to ask. I continued writing.

Will he try to talk me out of it? Probably. But I'll convince him to help me. I have to. Everything depends on it.

EIGHTEEN

*F*or once, I couldn't wait to get to school Monday morning. I didn't even try to argue with Mom when she reminded me to get in the car. The faster I got there, the better.

As we got near the drop off lane, I realized something was missing. Someone had taken down Bretta's sign . It made me sad, but only for a little while. I would keep my promise to Bretta, and I would stay strong so I could make things right. I jumped out of the car as soon as Mom pulled up to the curb.

I could hear her calling to me, so I turned to wave to her. She was mouthing something, but I couldn't hear her for the noise of an idling school bus. I waved back and went into the building. I headed for my locker, but that wasn't where I was going. When I turned the corner, I saw the person I needed. He was coming in the end door wheeling a dolly full of drinks. The hallway was pretty empty, and I was glad. I hurried over to him.

"Harvey, I need to talk to you," I whispered.

"Morning. You want a juice?" He reached for a peach bottle, but I shook my head.

"No, thanks. Harvey, I need your help."

"Sure. Glad to help." He wiped his hands on his pants leg and grinned. His grin faded when he looked in my eyes. It was pretty early, but a few kids, mostly teachers' aides, drifted by. I pretended to look over his selections as they moved around us. I waited until there was no one near enough to hear our conversation. Finally, the last kid shuffled away. I turned to Harvey. He was staring at me.

"Harvey, please don't say no," I started.

"What are you talking about?" he said, frowning. He was beginning to get a serious pucker between his eyes, too.

"I need your help. If you don't help me with this, I won't have anybody else, and I'll have to do it on my own. I don't think that's such a great idea, but if you won't help me ..." The words were spilling out so fast they were tripping all over each other as they fell out of my mouth. I stopped when he held up his hand.

"Whoa. Slow down, kid. Now, start over. You need my help with what?"

He crossed his arms and took a deep breath. The crease between his eyes went away—until I started outlining my plan. Then it returned and got deeper. They looked like a bottomless pit.

"Harvey, I think I know who killed Bretta." I was ready for his startled expression. I expected that. But, I dug in my heels and went on, telling him about Mrs. Bentley's daughter's death, as well as the van in her garage.

"Don't you see, Harvey? Did you know her daughter was murdered?" I lowered my voice so Mrs. Bentley couldn't hear me. Her door, even though it was closed, was only a few feet away from us. Harvey shook his head.

"Her daughter's murder was a LOT like Bretta's. They were about the same age. Tally was thirteen. Bretta had just turned fourteen. And their parents gave them anything they wanted. I'm sure Mrs. Bentley killed her daughter. She was the most important thing in the world to *Mr*. Bentley. I think Mrs. Bentley didn't like that, and she probably killed her husband, too. I'm telling you, Harvey, she's insane or something. When she looks at me, I can tell she hates me." I knew I sounded like a drama queen. But there wasn't time to explain all the information in detail. So I blundered on, telling him everything I knew about Tally and her death and my suspicions about Mrs. Bentley.

Harvey was shaking his head. But I was ready for that, too. I'd been awake most of the night planning my plea with Harvey. He had to help me. I said the one thing I knew would get to him.

"You have to help me. You know what it's like. You said yourself if you could have caught the person who killed your brother, you would have." He jerked like I'd hit a nerve. I hurried on. "This is the same thing. And ..." I hesitated.

"And what?" he prodded.

"And I've already set up a meeting with her," I said.

"You did what! Are you crazy? If you are right, and I don't think you are—but if you are right, then you're playing right into her hands. You can't do that. It's too dangerous. I *will not* have anything to do with this!" He turned his back and started shoving bottles and cans into the machine, placing one hand on his heart and rubbing.

I hung my head. Harvey was my only hope, and he was turning me down. Sighing, I turned and started to my locker. I had no idea what I was going to do without Harvey to back me up, but I would have to try and think of something. I hoisted my backpack and shrugged my shoulders.

"Wait a minute," he said. I stopped. Slowly, I turned and looked at him. Holding my breath, I waited. I didn't have to wait long.

"This is crazy. If she is the killer, then she's pretty smart," he whispered. "I mean she's gotten away with it now for six years. You're playing with fire, and you could get burned. Bad. Have you at least told the police what you think? You should go to them. This is their job!"

I shook my head. "No one knows but me. I started to tell someone, but," I shrugged. It was too embarrassing to tell Harvey my own father thought I was an immature child. "I didn't," I finished. "I promised Bretta I'd find her killer, and I'm keeping my promise—with your help, or without it." I jutted out my chin.

Harvey looked at the floor and then looked at me. A worry filled his face. "I don't like it. I mean, I know how you feel and all, but not telling the police or even your parents. This is not a good idea." He stuck his hands in his pockets and then looked me squarely in the eyes.

"I'm doing it, Harvey. And I'm not going to the police until I have evidence. I don't want to be laughed at."

"When are you supposed to meet her?"

"Tonight."

"That soon!" he quickly lowered his voice. Mr. Keely had been passing in the hall and glanced toward us.

"Yes, that soon," I said, whispering. "I'm not going to give her any more time to hurt anybody else. There's no telling how many times she's done this before that we don't even *know* about. You hear about people that have been serial killers for years and no one suspects them. Why else would she keep an old van all these years? I'm telling you, she uses it."

"What makes you think she has a van? What does that have to do with anything?"

"An eye witness thought he saw a van in the park about the time of Bretta's death, plus someone in a van followed me the other night on my way home."

"But you don't know for sure it was her," he insisted.

"Of course it was her. It's too much of a coincidence. Besides, she only lives three blocks from me. It would have been easy for her to follow me. Whether I meet her tonight or not, I'm in trouble. I'm pretty sure she knows I suspect her."

"I think you've been watching too many scary movies. You've lost your best friend, and you're under a lot of stress. Let's slow this thing down and …"

"No. I'm meeting her tonight under the bleachers."

His shoulders slumped. "What time?" he asked, running his hand across his head.

"So, are you going to help me or not?" I waited, not breathing. He stood there for a long time, just looking at me. Finally, he nodded.

"I'll do it. But—and I mean this. You don't get there one minute earlier than you're supposed to. I finish with my last run at 6:30. I'll come directly to the school and park somewhere out of the way, so she won't see me. I'll be there at seven, but don't come early. She probably will. I could get caught in traffic. You don't need to be there with her alone. Do you understand? I still think you should tell your parents," he said.

"Yeah. Okay. I understand. Whatever you say, Harvey. Thank you so much. You don't know what this means to me."

"Yes, I do," he nodded solemnly.

"Yeah. I guess you do." The bell rang, and the hall was full of teachers and students. I smiled at him gratefully and hurried to my locker. My heart felt ten times lighter than it had in days. Finally, I was going to make things right. Now, I had to figure out how to get through Bentley's class without throwing up.

As it turned out, I didn't have to worry. She was absent again. A new substitute filled in for her. She said she would cover material that would be on the next test which would be given when Mrs. Bentley returned. Everybody was in a great mood. Even Billy Isley answered questions, and that never happened. Some of his answers weren't very good, but that didn't stop him.

I sat bolt upright as I realized it couldn't be Billy who had pretended to be Bretta's Internet friend. The message I read last night had perfect grammar. Billy couldn't even string three sentences together, and his spelling was awful. That proved that Billy wasn't the murderer. Come to think of it, the texts pointed even more to Mrs. Bentley. The message was typed and spelled perfectly, like an English teacher had written it. Two pieces of the puzzle snapped into place. Bretta had said that "Regular Joe" looked like someone she should know.

And Dad said after the death of Tally and her father that Mrs. Bentley was all alone except for a brother. What if Regular Joe was Bentley's brother! There would probably be a resemblance. And Bretta had caught him *reading her posts in the chat room!* That meant he would have known how to contact her later in the chat room.

All of a sudden, everything that had happened made perfect sense. Bentley and her brother could have planned Tally's murder. Mr. Bentley's death had been called a heart attack, but had it really been that or could it have been something else? Dad said she received life insurance. Maybe she shared it with her brother. The regular guy Bretta saw looked familiar because he looked like his sister, Mrs. Bentley!

The rest of the day dragged on. By seventh period I was a wreck. I dropped my books outside Mr. Peterson's door and tromped all over Pam's feet in the hall. I dropped a jar of paint in Mrs. Watson's class and shelved three books in the wrong place in the library. I had to get a grip. It didn't help that the sky was getting dark, and thunder kept rolling overhead. The temperature was dropping. Someone said there was a chance of storms later tonight. Great.

By the time the last bell rang, I knew I'd never make it without totally freaking out if I didn't calm myself down. So, the minute Mom and I got home, I went straight to my room and started doing just that. I picked up my journal and began to write. Writing *always* calmed me.

I outlined my whole plan. My meeting place, the time, and what I was taking with me. By the time I finished, I was okay and, in a weird way, peaceful.

I wanted Bretta's shoes. I wasn't sure why, but I wanted them on my feet when I faced Mrs. Bentley. It seemed right somehow. Pulling them on, I laced them up and tied a second knot in them. The last thing I needed was to stumble or trip.

Sitting at my desk, I started jotting down other things. I doodled for a while, drawing a picture of the bleachers and making a banner that sort of looked like the one the girls' basketball team had hung up. The sketch had Bretta's name on it, but I sketched in a little clock with the hands pointing to seven. Sometimes doodling helped me think.

My sketch worked this time. My mind kicked into high gear, and I started gathering things to take with me and statements I needed to say to Bentley when I had her within range of my cell phone. I planned to put it into record mode before I got to the bleachers. Then, I could catch everything she said.

I had to get her to confess. That should be easy. She wouldn't think about me recording what we said.

The hard part would be getting her to the police. Would she simply give up once she realized I had her confession recorded? I doubted it. Harvey had said that she had gotten away with it for years, and she wasn't likely to just throw her hands up and go along. Like any criminal, she'd fight to get away. Would I be able to stand up to her? What if Harvey didn't get there? What if something happened? What if. What if. What if. I glanced in the direction of Dad's room. Maybe Harvey was right. Maybe I should tell Dad what I was planning. But even as I thought it, I knew he would absolutely forbid me from doing it. And then what? I'd have to live with the guilt of Bretta's death for the rest of my life. No way. A fuzzy thought nagged at my brain, but it fluttered away too quickly for me to grasp it. Oh, well. It wouldn't be long before everything was on track again. The guilt would finally go away.

Then another thought—a solid one, tumbled into my brain. I should take something else with me. Some sort of weapon in case Harvey didn't show. I looked around the room for something I could stick in my pocket. It would have to be something light that wouldn't show and wouldn't slow me down. My eyes roamed around the room a couple of times. They landed on the perfect thing. It was the charcoal pencil Bretta had used to sketch my picture. She had taped it to the bottom of the picture as her "signature." She intended to do that with all of her pieces when she became famous.

I walked to the picture and carefully took the pencil from the tape holding it in place. She put it right under her real signature, like an underscore. I smiled. And then I sharpened it to a fine, sharp point. I placed it my pocket with my cell.

After an hour, my list was complete, and my heart and mind had calmed.

I was ready for my meeting with Bretta's killer.

NINETEEN

I had some trouble getting away from the house. After dinner, Mom and Aunt Jane wanted me to help them dig out all the candles in case the lights went out because of the predicted storm. Since we used up most of our candles the night of the break-in, they decided to go to the store and get more. They practically begged me to go with them, but I told them I had to study. It wasn't a lie. I had to study my plan for meeting with Bentley. That left Dad to deal with. He skipped dinner and stayed in his room. That was okay by me. The clock was ticking toward six twenty.

"I'm going over to Pam's to study, Dad," I yelled up the stairs. That *was* a lie.

"On a Monday?" he called back. He stepped to the door and peered down at me.

"Yep. I won't be gone long." Then I told him a flat-out huge lie. "Pam's mom is picking me up." He hesitated. My heart started pounding. What was I going to do if he said no?

"I'll be home in about an hour or so." He disappeared back into his room. I moved from one foot to the other. What was he doing? I looked at my watch. Six thirty. My hand was on the knob.

"Wait a minute. Here, take my cell with you, honey. Yours could always go dead. I don't want to take any chances. The battery could be low. Call me when you get ready to leave, and I'll pick you up." He smiled and came down the stairs. "I'm sorry about what happened, Rachel. I was out of line. I love you. I hope you know that. I…" he choked on his words. "I haven't said that much lately."

I almost caved right there and told him where I was going. I wanted him to be with me and be proud of me when I finally made Bretta's killer confess.

But I knew he wouldn't allow me. He'd feel like I was doing something too dangerous. Or maybe he'd tell me again how childish I was being. I couldn't stand to hear that again. I just nodded, "I know, Dad." A crash of lightning made me jump. "I think I hear her already. I'll see you in a little while." I smiled again and waved at him from the door. Stepping outside, I took a long, deep breath and prayed hard that he wouldn't look outside. I pulled my hood up over my head and felt around for the flashlight I stuck in my pocket with my cell phone. I pulled Dad's out and programmed 911 into speed dial. I put it back in the pocket with Bretta's pencil. The metal from the flashlight was cold, and its weight bothered me, but it was the only one I could find with batteries that worked.

The sky was dark, and clouds were hovering. I figured the storm wasn't far away. I hoped with all my heart Harvey would not change his mind. I'd needed his help.

Some kind of electrical charge was in the air. It made every step more determined. I hurried from one block to the next. The thunder overhead matched the thudding of my heart. I checked the time again. Six forty-seven. I was only a block away from school when the first fat raindrop hit my face. It was cold, and the wind whipped my jacket. I was glad I wore gloves, but looking down, I realized I probably shouldn't have worn canvas shoes. Bretta's shoes were already soaked.

I rounded the corner and looked at the front of the school. Everything looked the same as it had when I left today, except the traffic. The grounds were deserted—except for one vehicle. It was

Mrs. Bentley's green Mercedes. Did she have the van parked somewhere else? Was it near the bleachers? The gym and track weren't far away. Had she parked it in the wooded area behind the gym? I was sure that's where the van would be. I decided to take the long way around to see if I could spot the van in the woods.

I wore black, thinking it would blend into the night. Now, I was glad I had. No one could see me hugging edges of the woods, but I didn't want to go too near in case Bentley was there.

I rounded a clearing— and saw it. In the dimming light, all I could see was the shape of a big vehicle. But it was the van, and it was large, and it was parked in an isolated area. The back panel door was open. I stopped dead. Was Bentley in there? Something was smeared on the door. Thunder rumbled overhead. I looked at my watch and hurried toward the bleachers. I was hoping I could slip up on her. With all the thunder overhead, that should be easy. Lightning ripped across the sky and lit up the football field. I froze, hunkering behind a nearby sign. I checked my cell one last time. Six fifty-seven. It was time. Peeking out from behind the tree, I scanned the bleachers. I couldn't see anyone. Not even Harvey. Had he forgotten? Had he decided not to come? But he had said to get there at exactly 7:00.

I stood and started making my way toward the bleachers. As I got near them, I could see a light shining in Bentley's classroom. Was she still in there? The shades were pulled. I bet she deliberately arranged them so nobody could see inside. To anybody passing by, it would look like she was just another dedicated teacher working late.

I reached in my pocket to make sure Bretta's pencil was still there. I programmed my cell phone to record. I hadn't told Bentley at which end of the bleachers I'd be, but that was okay. She'd find me.

Taking the flashlight out of my pocket, I switched it on. I could always shine it in her face and blind her if she came at me too fast. That would give me time to grab the pencil. But I had to get her confession first. I had to have time to talk to her.

Hearing a noise to my left, I whirled around, expecting to see her. I turned the flashlight off. Then I did something really brilliant. I dropped it. It rolled down the incline. I turned back toward the school and saw her tall, skinny frame as it walked out the door and down the sidewalk.

She stopped and cocked her head, listening. Had she heard the clank of the flashlight? I watched as she made her way toward the car. I heard the door unlock. She glanced back once in my direction then was behind her wheel and pulling out of the parking lot and onto the street that led toward her house. There was movement behind me.

Jumping, I turned around. I saw Harvey's smiling face.

"You scared me half to death," I said, my voice shaking. I looked at Harvey. He was watching Bentley drive away. I watched, too. And I was totally confused. Frowning, I looked at Harvey.

"You were sure it was her, weren't you?" he asked.

I nodded. "I'm still sure it's her. It can't be Billy Isley. I've completely ruled him out, and I don't for one second believe it was a stranger. It has to be Mrs. Bentley. All the pieces fit. This has to be a trick. Either that or she's chickened out." My next thought hit me like a rock. Bentley wouldn't have driven her car *and* brought the van that was in the woods. That wouldn't make sense. Too many people could see her. I felt the hair on the back of my neck begin to stiffen.

"It wasn't her, Rachel," Harvey said, quietly. "It was never her."

Harvey's voice sounded strange. When I studied his face I froze when I saw the odd look in his eyes. He was smiling, but it wasn't his friendly lopsided smile. This smile was slow and mean. Chilling.

Oddly, my mind remembered a passage from one of the Holocaust books about maniacs and their bad deeds and the smiles that went with them. I never thought I'd see one …

I tried to back away, but it was like my feet were nailed to the ground. Harvey started walking toward me. I looked in the direction of the parking lot. Deserted. My only hope just drove away. How could I have been so wrong?

"I knew she'd leave about now," Harvey said, grinning. "She always leaves about now when she's getting lesson plans ready for a sub. Doesn't like to be up here alone, you know." He chuckled. "That's why I suggested 7:00. Witnesses will recall seeing her vehicle here until right about now. So, it's quite possible she might get blamed for your death. That would be perfect. Her husband got blamed for Tally's death six years ago. Now it will be her turn." He grinned.

"How did you know Tally had died six years ago?" I asked, but I already knew the truth.

"How do you think I knew?" he asked. He cocked his head and gestured with his hand. "Go on," he taunted. "Tell me what you think?"

"I think you killed her."

He bowed. "I did."

"Was she the first person you killed?"

"No. She was the second. The first was my brother."

I gasped. "But you said he was hit by a car," I stammered.

"He was. I threw that ball right in front of it. He never saw the car coming. That was easy.

"Bretta's murder took a bit more planning. A chat room was perfect. She was so stupid, and she did make it easy—almost too easy. She groused one day about not having a phone of her own because she wanted to chat about art. I suggested one my friend's kid used." He grinned. "I don't have any friends."

The look he gave me made my blood run cold.

I stared at him. I couldn't believe what was happening. Sweet, innocent Harvey was a cold-blooded killer. Harvey, whom everyone trusted and talked to, was a murderer. All this time, he'd been right there. Visible. Ordinary. Trusted. He was part of my daily life.

"Why did you do those things?" I whispered.

"Why not?"

It wouldn't bother him to kill me. Another clap of thunder sounded over our heads. He never took his eyes off me. I remembered the pencil in my pocket. He didn't know about that. He didn't know about my cell phone either. I prayed it was getting all this. I took a step back. He took a step forward. There were only a few yards between us.

I needed to keep him talking. "I don't understand, Harvey. A person doesn't do things like that just because he can. There has to be a reason."

He shrugged. "I was sick of my brother," he said hatefully. "Until he came along, my life was perfect. I was an only child. My parents doted on me. Then he," he fairly spit the word out of his mouth, "came along. He ruined everything. I thought that once he was gone, things would go back to the way they had been, but it was never the same after that. My parents were never right after that. When I grew up, I went away, and things got better. But when they died, they left me the house that was here so I came back. I started working this job," he said. "The school was on my route, and I started noticing certain kids. Brats like him that were spoiled. Tally was one of those."

"But her parents loved her. Don't you feel anything?" I shouted.

He frowned, and I was afraid he'd lunge, but instead, he stood very still. "No. I don't think I do," he said, pursing his lips. He looked up and cocked his head. "No." He shook his head. "I don't feel guilty about getting rid of problems. That's what I do. I get rid of problems." He took another step toward me. I backed up. He stopped. "I was pretty proud of the way I lured Bretta into meeting me," he bragged. "Do you know what I did?"

I shook my head. I wasn't sure I wanted to know all of it, but I needed to stall for time.

"I'd watched her for over a year. I knew everywhere she went, who she visited, even when she went to that little coffee shop.

"I walked by the café one day, and Bretta was on the computer. "I started wearing a disguise. She never even suspected it was me. I started noticing that she was really bad about leaving her page up when she got up to do something.

"YOU were the guy that sat down at her computer and was reading her stuff!"

Harvey chuckled. "That's right, sweetheart. I was "regular guy. "

It was all so easy. I can't believe how stupid people are. I set up a fake screen identity, and she never even knew it was me. Sometimes, I even chatted with her from *in* the cafe. She never suspected a thing. She thought she was so smart. She was an idiot."

"I was careful about the possibility of my stuff being traced. I'm pretty good at computers," he bragged. Straightening his shoulders, he cleared his throat. "I deliberately came after school one day to service the drink machines. It was a piece of cake convincing the custodian I had trouble with one of them. I gave him a sob story about how I was dead-tired and running late and needed to send my boss an e-mail. Mrs. Bentley's room is the closest one to the machines, so I just asked to use that one. In no time at all, I was on her computer with my flash drive, installing software that would let me access her computer any time I wanted—from anywhere. I knew if the police ever did trace the e-mails, it would lead them to her."

I was stunned.

"Pretty impressive, huh, Rachel? You probably thought I was some dummy who couldn't get a better job, didn't you? I'm not. I'm very smart," he sneered. "The only time I messed up was not disconnecting service to that stupid cell phone I had sent to Bretta."

Swallowing hard, I pressed him. "I don't understand, Harvey. Why did you answer?"

"Because now you're a risk. I knew you weren't going to stop snooping around. You *should* have left this alone, Rachel. I told you it was dangerous. You should have listened. Now, I have to take care of another problem. You."

"But, why Bretta?" I hedged.

"Because she had everything and didn't even appreciate it. Tally was the same way. Both of them were spoiled brats," he spat.

"What about Tally's father? Didn't it bother you he suffered so much he had a heart attack?"

"He didn't have a heart attack because of Tally. He had a heart attack because I put something in his drink. Even *his* murder was brilliant. I told you. I'm very good at what I do.

"I waited for a day when Isabel had a meeting. Her husband was alone, working in that garage shop of his. He was a natural snoop, like you. I could tell he had started to suspect something, and I was afraid he might find out the truth. Really, I had no choice. I couldn't let Mr. Bentley's interference ruin me. I had to take care of the problem.

"I started spying on him. That's when I noticed he always took a big glass of something into the shop with him to drink while he worked. All I had to do was watch for him to step inside the house. When he did, I slipped some of my nitroglycerin pills into his drink. The police never suspected a thing. And even if they had, they probably would have suspected his wife. You did."

I remembered seeing Harvey rub his chest. It never registered he had heart problems and was probably taking medicine for it. Shaking my head, I felt so bad as I imagined Mr. Bentley dying all alone in his shop, never knowing what had happened to his daughter. I'd been so ready to blame Mrs. Bentley for both deaths! Shame washed over me—and fear. *Please, God. I need help.*

Night crept in around us. I knew if I tried to run, Harvey would catch me. He was bigger, stronger, and probably faster. I couldn't get a lot of traction in Bretta's rain-soaked shoes. He'd have no problem taking me out.

"What about the van?" I stalled. Maybe in the dark, he wouldn't see me edging away from him. He shifted. I moved another inch away.

"The van in the woods is mine. I saw you looking at it. It's my old delivery truck. I keep it parked in a storage building for safekeeping. I have a new one now, but I keep the old one in case I need it—like tonight. I used it on the night when it was foggy, too, but your friends almost saw it."

"That was you!"

"Sure was," he bragged. "Like I said, you were getting too nosy. I was waiting for you. Even saw that Isley kid when he went in your house. Thought for a little while he was going to take away my fun."

I'd been right about Billy breaking in. Just wrong about him hurting Bretta. "But the van I saw in Mrs. Bentley's garage?" I started.

"That's the old van her husband used. Isn't it sweet? She never could bear to part with it. This has worked out very well. Once you're dead, I intend to plant some of your blood in it. The police are already looking for a van. They'll get an anonymous tip from a helpful citizen telling them to check old Mrs. Bentley's garage."

"Why are you doing this to her?" I demanded.

"Because it will take the blame away from me." He placed his hand in his pocket and pulled out something small. I heard a click and saw the glint of something. I was pretty sure it was a knife. I sucked in my breath and wished I'd told someone else where I was going. I would never get to tell Dad how much I loved him or explain to Mom and Aunt Jane why I did this incredibly stupid thing.

"I told my parents."

"No, you didn't," he smiled, shaking his head. "I followed you. I had to be sure in case you decided to take my *sincere* advice. But I knew you wouldn't. You had something to prove. Nope. You came alone. Dad is probably stretched out in his easy chair, and your mom and aunt have had a convenient flat. I made sure of that by putting a slow leak in their tire."

I blinked. What if the tire blew out? What if they skidded off the road? What if they were hurt, or worse? It would be my fault. Just like Bretta's death had been my fault. Anger surged inside me. Reaching in my pocket, I touched the pencil—and dad's cell phone. With thunder rumbling loudly overhead, I punched what I hoped was the right speed dial button.

"Now, it's time to get this over with, Rachel," Harvey said, raising his voice to be heard over the thunder. "I don't have all night." He began walking toward me. I backed up, but then my back hit the cold, hard metal of the supporting beam. I was trapped. I pulled out the pencil.

"What's that?" he asked harshly. "What are you holding?"

"I'm not stupid, either, Harvey. I brought a weapon with me."

Silence filled the night air. Rain began beating against the metal of the bleachers. Little of it hit us, but the wind was whipping at my jacket, and my teeth began to chatter. Out of the corner of my eye, I caught sight of something

Harvey lunged at me, his knife grazing my hand. Turning quickly, I stepped around the metal beam toward the opening behind me. Harvey's strong hands closed around my throat. I felt his breath, hot and fast, on my cheek. Closing my eyes, I plunged Bretta's pencil into his hand and listened as he shrieked. Stunned, I watched him pull it out and hold it up as the lightning flashed again overhead. In that second, I saw Mrs. Bentley. She was standing behind Harvey. Her dress was plastered to her thin frame and her fists clenched, and her jaw a jagged edge of fury. Then she jumped him from behind. Surprised, he looked at me, not understanding who had attacked him. Immediately he began trying to toss her off his back. But with her arms tightening around his neck, he began to stumble.

"*You* did it!" she screamed. "You killed my little girl and my husband, you monster!"

For a split second, I just stood there watching the scene in front of me. Pure, scorching anger had attached itself to Harvey's back.

Harvey wrenched himself to the right, trying to dislodge her hold on him. He dropped the knife and then fell to his knees, stretching his hand toward the weapon. He pushed his fingers as far as they would reach to touch the blade. Without thinking, I ran to the knife and kicked it out of his reach. Then I kicked him in the stomach.

"You witch!" he snarled. Frenzied with rage, he whirled in a circle and began limping toward one of the heavy supporting steel beams. I couldn't figure out what he was doing. Then with a sickening understanding, I knew. He began running backward toward the beam. Even with the storm raging, I heard the impact and watched as Mrs. Bentley crumpled to the ground. I watched as Harvey raised his heavy, boot-clad foot and took aim at her chest.

I grabbed the flashlight on the ground and ran toward him. Taking dead aim, I hit his head with all my strength. Grunting, he fell to the ground, not moving. Mrs. Bentley tried to sit up, but grabbed her ribs and moaned. Then, seeing Harvey lying beside her, she wrenched the flashlight out of my hand. Raising her hand above her head, I saw the desperation in her eyes. Shaking, she glared at the man responsible for her misery.

He moaned, and for a split second, she hesitated, her resolve weakening. The beam from the flashlight danced around in the darkness, and then it lit up a face. Dad's face. He grabbed the flashlight from her hand, and lunged on top of Harvey, landing squarely on his chest. Within seconds, Harvey's hands were behind his back.

I reached out for Mrs. Bentley, taking her hand. She was trembling almost as much as I was. Together, we sat on the wet ground and watched as the man responsible for so many deaths was dragged to his feet and placed inside a police car.

"How did you know I was here?" I asked.

"I heard a noise as I was leaving," she said, holding her side. She winced. Harvey must have broken some of her ribs when he slammed her into the post. "At first, I thought it was probably only kids, but something about it nagged at me, so I decided to drive around and come in the back way through the woods." She blew out a soft breath and closed her eyes. I knew she was in pain. I couldn't tell if it was from her injury or something else.

"Then you saw the van, didn't you?" I asked, still holding one of her hands. Her hair was clinging to her head, and she looked so thin, almost frail.

"Yes," she whispered. "When I saw it, I was confused. It looked so much like the one my husband used to drive," she sighed. "I began looking more closely and realized it was an old vending truck. I couldn't come up with a reasonable explanation as to why the vending man would park in the woods. Then I remembered the police report about seeing a van in the park the day Bretta died."

"That's when I became concerned." She shrugged painfully. "I never have gotten around to getting a cell phone. It was a lavish expense I've always thought I could do without. When I spotted that van, I'd have given anything for one, but—since I didn't have one I knew I wouldn't have time to make it to a phone. Instead, I tried to get to the bleachers as quickly as I could, but I knew I had to be quiet." she explained. "The thunder helped camouflage my movements. He never knew I was there until I jumped him." She smiled, a look of tired triumph in her eyes. "By then, he was explaining how he had killed my family." She swallowed hard. "I wanted to kill him." She stopped and looked at me defiantly.

I nodded. "I don't blame you," I whispered. "I even thought you were going to when you got hold of the flashlight."

"I couldn't do it. I guess that makes me weak, but I couldn't take another human's life," she said, looking at the leaden sky. "Thank God," she said.

For a few moments, we both listened to the commotion taking place on the field. Harvey was shouting while one of the police officers was reading him his rights.

"I know why you didn't kill him," I said. "Because you're not like him. We both hate what he is, and what he did, but we're not like him."

Mrs. Bentley dropped her head. I couldn't tell if she was crying or just trying to get a grip on everything that had happened. Either way, she needed a few minutes to get herself collected. I sat beside her. Then I heard a familiar voice. It was a very loud voice, but one I was thrilled to hear.

"Rachel," Mom shouted. "Where are you?" I could see Mom running frantically toward Dad in the parking lot. Her car door was flung open, and I noticed that one of her tires was completely flat. Her footsteps were slapping the wet asphalt. Aunt Jane was right behind her.

"I'm over here, Mom." She skidded around the steel pole. Kneeling, she put her arms around me. I looked at Dad as he came behind her.

"Mrs. Bentley needs an ambulance," I told them. "She's hurt." But Mom was looking at me. The cut made from Harvey's knife had made a large slice in my hand that I hadn't paid much attention to because of everything else that had happened. Blood was all over my clothes. Looking down, I saw a lot of blood on Bretta's shoes. The blood from the cut, mixed with the rain, had left them a sickly pink/red color.

Their image swam before my eyes and was the last thing I saw before I fainted.

TWENTY

*M*rs. Bentley and I both ended up in the emergency room. The doctors insisted she stay overnight, but I wanted to go home. After stitching the cut, which ended up being pretty deep, they let me go. During the ride I was fuzzy. Aunt Jane and Mom were on either side of me. Dad was driving his car. The shot for pain they gave me made me fall asleep on the couch as soon as we got home.

When I woke up, the fire was crackling, and Mom, Aunt Jane and Dad were sitting around me talking. Edna was purring in my face. I tried to sit up, but all four of them nearly had a fit. Even Edna gently slapped my face when I tried to sit up.

"Stay still," Mom ordered. Worry was written all over her face. Aunt Jane and Dad looked pretty much the same.

I nodded. "My hand hurts," I said, dropping my head. "And I feel stupid."

None of them disagreed with me. Aunt Jane took my good hand and squeezed it. "Why on earth did you do this?"

"You didn't think you were confronting Harvey, did you?" Dad asked.

I shook my head and wondered how he knew. "I thought I was setting up a meeting with Mrs. Bentley," I said. I knew they deserved the whole ugly truth, so I started by telling them about Bretta and the

171

chat room then all the rest of it started tumbling out of my mouth.

I ended by explaining how I watched Mrs. Bentley drive out of the parking lot. "Even then, I was sure she had done it and was just trying to fool me. It never occurred to me Harvey could have been the killer. He set Bretta up, Dad," I said, turning to him. Edna slapped at me again, and I slumped back against the cushions on the couch.

"He knew everything about her because he was the one chatting with her online!"

"Well, Harvey's plan worked," Aunt Jane said. "He lured that girl to her death."

"Yeah," I said, still rubbing my head. "It worked. But it wouldn't have if I hadn't gone along with it."

Finally. I'd said the words.

Silence surrounded me. I closed my eyes, and tears slid down my face. "I'm so ashamed. If I'd told Bretta I wouldn't cover for her when she went to meet Harvey, she'd be alive." I felt Dad's strong arms around my shoulders.

"If Harvey hadn't killed Bretta then, he would have found another way or another person. He's a sadistic, cold-blooded killer, and he targeted Bretta just like he did Tally and her father. You didn't cause Bretta's death."

"But I could have stopped Bretta that day," I said, wiping the tears from my eyes.

"Yes, you could have," Dad said. "But more than likely, she would have met him another time. Bretta should never have been in a chat room. They're open to everybody, and you never know if the person you're chatting with is really who they say they are. A lot of pedophiles use them as charting stations. They target the kid they want and then make a chart about them. As the kid posts information, it's charted; their age, what they like, their hobbies, even where they work. Sometimes kids even post where they live. Sometimes it's right in their screen name. Then, when the chart's complete, the stalker starts to hunt them down. That's why we don't want you to go into chat rooms."

I nodded miserably. But Harvey wasn't a stalker."

"Yes, he was. It just happened to be one who Bretta knew."

"I thought I could make the guilt go away if I could find her killer," I said lamely.

"Well, you did find Bretta's killer," Dad said. "But what you did could have gotten you killed, Kitten. It was incredibly irresponsible, but," he said, tilting his head, "I have to admit that because of your recorder idea, we have his confession. Since it's a murder case, we can use it in court, but I suspect he'll confess on his own. A lot of serial killers enjoy bragging about their crimes. Until now, we had no evidence linking either girl's death or Mr. Bentley's to Harvey, so the recording is our ace in the hole.

And—you need to stop blaming just yourself for Bretta's death. You've got to remember that if she hadn't set up a meeting, he would have figured out some other way to get to her. There're any number of ways to talk to someone these days—and criminals know them all. That's why he sent her the phone."

Nodding, I let all that sink in. But I knew if I'd just told someone, her secret would have been out. Then what happened would have been out of my hands. I'd always carry some of the guilt. I'd have to live with that. But I had my family to help, and I had God. I needed to start listening to Him instead of just asking for things.

Edna jumped up beside me and curled into a little ball. I turned to Dad.

"How did you know where I was?"

"Pam called," he said.

I groaned. It never occurred to me to ask Pam to cover for me. But then I would have been putting her in the same position I'd been in when Bretta asked me to lie for her.

He patted my hand. "Once I realized you weren't at her house, I was sick with worry. My gut told me you were in trouble, so I went to your room. I snooped. I found your journal."

"I'm glad you did," I smiled.

"Me, too," he said. "I'm glad you keep a hard copy journal, honey."

"Then," Mom said, "when he realized you set up a meeting, he called the person you'd written about, Mrs. Bentley. When she didn't answer, he called the police and then headed to the school. The dispatcher said they'd already received a 911 transmission. I guess that's the one you placed when you realized you were in trouble. That was very good thinking," Mom said proudly. "Anyway, Steve called me just before he left to go to school. I got there as fast as I could, flat tire and all."

"When we arrived, I couldn't see you, and I panicked," Dad said. "Then I saw Mrs. Bentley attacking someone. At first, I thought it was you but when I got closer, I realized she was on somebody else."

"Mrs. Bentley's a brave woman," Mom said. "She didn't have any idea what she was going to encounter when she got there. She just knew someone might need her help. I'm glad she got there when she did."

I nodded, thinking how much I owed the woman I had suspected of murdering her daughter and husband. I looked at each of them. "I'm sorry," I repeated. "I wanted to make things right, but the way I did things was all wrong. Plus, I got Mrs. Bentley hurt. I didn't do any of this the right way."

"I understand," Dad said, nodding. He looked at Aunt Jane. "That feeling can eat you up if you let it. But sometimes you have to accept that your actions have consequences, and we can't go back and undo what's happened. We can't run away from it, either. We just have to trust in God and do his will. That's something I haven't been very good at either."

Dad reached over and put his arm around Aunt Jane. She reached back and held onto him. Mom smiled and patted me on the leg. Edna purred.

I sat on the edge of my bed later that night and picked up my dictionary. As I began thumbing through the pages, I sighed, relieved that the ordeal was over and Harvey was behind bars.

Reaching the J pages, I ran my fingers from one word to the next. I wanted to put things to rest. I flipped through a lot of pages. There it was. The perfect word.

Juncture: Point in time, one made critical or important by circumstances. I began to write.

Monday p.m. 9:50

Dad's been on the phone a lot tonight. People are calling to find out what happened and to see if we're okay. He had a phone call from the precinct saying Harvey had confessed everything, even about Tally Bentley and her father. He is a sick man.

Mom and Aunt June are downstairs talking to Dad right now. I'm thinking it would be nice if he stayed.

*I'm a little surprised I still miss Bretta. Even though she wasn't the person I thought she was, she didn't deserve to die the way she did. The guilt's not as bad, but I don't think it will ever go away. That's something I'll have to deal with, and maybe that's the way it's supposed to be. I shouldn't have agreed to cover for her—and she shouldn't have asked me to. I guess I always figured things would just go on and on. But, it doesn't always. It can end on a bright, sunny day. For now, at this **juncture** I'll just appreciate what I have—and what I've lost.*

www.ingramcontent.com/pod-product-compliance
Lightning Source LLC
Chambersburg PA
CBHW030158200626
46812CB00017B/2691